*'I'm Beginning to
Think I Made a
Mistake in Marrying You.'*

'Already?' He held her from him, his eyes
troubled.

'Carlos,' she began huskily, 'I—' She stopped
abruptly, gasping in surprise as he drew her
tightly into his embrace, and before she could
even guess at his intention he was kissing her.
For a stunned and disbelieving moment she
was robbed of the ability either to move or
think, and she remained passive in his arms
while his lips possessed hers, moist and
sensuous and thrillingly masterful. As quivers
of longing rippled through Hydee's whole
body, she heard him whisper hoarsely,
'Hydee . . . my wife. . . .'

ANNE HAMPSON
currently makes her home in Ireland, but this
top romance author has traveled and lived all
over the world. This variety of experience is
reflected in her books, which present the ever-
changing face of romance as it is found wherever people fall in love.

Dear Reader:

Silhouette Romances is an exciting new publishing venture. We will be presenting the very finest writers of contemporary romantic fiction as well as outstanding new talent in this field. It is our hope that our stories, our heroes and our heroines will give you, the reader, all you want from romantic fiction.

Also, *you* play an important part in our future plans for Silhouette Romances. We welcome any suggestions or comments on our books and I invite you to write to us at the address below.

So, enjoy this book and all the wonderful romances from Silhouette. They're for *you!*

Karen Solem
Editor-in-Chief
Silhouette Books
P.O. Box 769
New York, N.Y. 10019

ANNE HAMPSON
Fascination

Silhouette *Romance*

Published by Silhouette Books New York

America's Publisher of Contemporary Romance

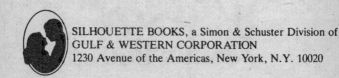 SILHOUETTE BOOKS, a Simon & Schuster Division of
GULF & WESTERN CORPORATION
1230 Avenue of the Americas, New York, N.Y. 10020

ISBN: 0-671-57108-7

First Silhouette Books printing October, 1981

10 9 8 7 6 5 4 3 2 1

Map by Tony Ferrara

America's Publisher of Contemporary Romance

Printed in the U.S.A.

Fascination

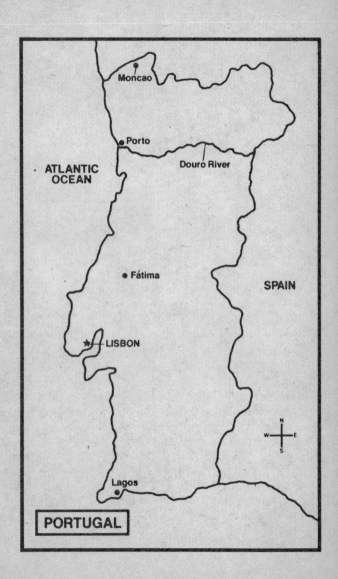

Chapter One

Shadows lingered in the silver-spangled half-dusk,
blending to obscure the last dying rays of sunlight as
they sank behind the darkened hills. To the south the
sea, caught in the afterglow, made a gentle play of
light and shade as its waves rippled onto the drowsy
waterfront. On the bridge stood a girl, a lone figure
staring down at the foaming river as it made its way
to the sea. Her dark hair, stirred by the breeze, fell
onto her face and she lifted a hand to brush it aside,
her eyes brooding and dull, her heart devoid of feeling, but in her mind the article she had read in the
newspaper that morning. Noel Carrington, gifted
manager of the White Hart in Crady-on-Sea, had
been promoted and was to take over the manage-

ment of the five-star hotel just built by the Condon Group—the Nelson at Lynport.

Hydee Merrill and Noel Carrington. . . . It seemed a million years since their names had been linked, since their engagement had been broken when Noel had fallen in love with someone else and had asked Hydee for his ring back. A million years, and yet it was only just over a year. Hydee had been twenty-three at the time and Noel twenty-nine.

'My girl,' her friend asked her half an hour after she had left the bridge, 'where have you been? As if I didn't know. Standing on that bridge, staring down into the river and seeing yourself drowned. But I'm never anxious about you, Hydee, because I know you better than you know yourself. You've far too much strength of character to take the easy way out.' Ellie switched on an extra lamp and moved it closer to the sideboard where she was carving a small joint of beef. She and Hydee had been sharing a flat for just over two years but they had been colleagues for almost four, ever since Ellie had come to work in the same office as Hydee. 'Go and change, love. It's Saturday, and you know we always make a big thing of dinner. I've put the wine to cool in the fridge and the vegetables and sweet are almost ready.'

'I haven't helped a bit.'

'You did all the weekend chores this morning while I was viewing that house. I think it'll suit Ray and me, as I told you, but I'll have to wait till he comes home before I dare make a final decision.'

'If he likes the house, you'll be married before Christmas?'

Ellie paused, the knife idle in her hand. She was troubled about her friend and yet excited at the prospect of getting married and setting up house with her beloved Ray. He was a travelling salesman at present but intended to change his job once he and Ellie were married.

'I expect Ray will want to be married as soon as possible,' she said at length. 'If we settle for that house, though, we'll need several weeks to get it ready for occupation. You can imagine what it's like, with that aged spinster living in it for the past forty-three years—not that she was aged at first,' amended Ellie in some amusement. She hoped to make Hydee laugh, and she succeeded.

'No, I don't suppose she was. However, to be serious, it must be a shambles if it looks anything like what you described. But if you can get it cheaply, then it'll be well worth the trouble of doing it up. It's certainly in a nice area, and it's a good size.'

Hydee went up to her room, washed in the pretty blue basin, put on a long skirt of flowered cotton with a crisp white blouse and used some blusher and lipstick. Then she took a long look at herself in the mirror before going downstairs to join her friend in the room that served as both living and dining room.

They were having dinner when Hydee said, as casually as she could, 'Noel's being moved to Lynport. He's been made manager of that fabulous new hotel they've built there, the Nelson.'

'How nice,' said Ellie in a brittle tone.

'He'll have a super flat in the hotel, I expect.'

'For himself and his wife, eh?'

Hydee nodded, and for a moment concentrated on the delicious beef which Ellie had put onto her plate. She regretted mentioning Noel, of whom Ellie always spoke with the utmost contempt, but Hydee could not always refrain from mentioning him; it seemed at times that something carried her on a tide of memory, and for a brief spell he would be hers again.

'I've been thinking, Ellie,' murmured Hydee, cutting herself a piece of meat, 'that when you've gone I shall get myself a job with children.'

'With children?' Ellie frowned, faintly startled. 'Why?'

'Well, I'm sure I'll never get married, and as I love children, I'd like to get a job looking after some.'

Ellie's frown deepened. 'Of course you'll get married, Hydee!'

'No, I'd never even look at another man. I'm not risking anything like that again.'

'It wouldn't happen again.'

'You're not in a position to say. Anyway, I'm not risking it. I'm staying single and getting myself a job like I've mentioned.'

'You mean you'd like to be a nursemaid or something?' said Ellie, exasperated.

'Yes, that's right. I don't want to live alone when you've gone, and if I get the post of nanny, I'll live as one of the family.'

Ellie was far too impatient to pursue the matter, and she changed the subject, deliberately steering her friend's thoughts to something else, and the meal was eaten in an atmosphere of pleasant talk and companionship.

'I was lucky having you at the time Noel threw me over,' murmured Hydee, breaking a lull in the conversation. 'I don't know what I'd have done without you. It isn't as if I've any relatives.' Her thoughts winged to that terrible day when her father's employer had come to the door to tell her that her father had died of a heart attack while at work.

12

She had still been at school at the time, barely eighteen, and had been left totally alone in the world, her mother having died four years previously. Her father's boss had been wonderful, giving her a well-paid post in his office and renting her a flat cheaply in one of the modern blocks he owned.

'Are you really serious about getting another job?' It was very plain that Ellie hated the idea of her friend spending all her days looking after someone else's children.

'Yes, I'm quite serious.'

'I feel bad about leaving you, Hydee.'

'Then you shouldn't. I've had your companionship for two years, and I'm grateful. We'll still remain good friends, and I know I'll always be welcome in your home.' Hydee looked at her and smiled, trying to shake her out of her sudden dejection. 'You know, Ellie, you're the only real friend I've ever had since my father died. When I got myself settled in this flat after selling up our little home, I had a girl to share who didn't seem able to get along with me at all. I feel it was my fault—'

'I'll bet it wasn't! Anyone could get along with you who was in the least compatible.'

'Well, whatever the reason, we found ourselves getting on one another's nerves from the start. After she left, I had someone else, and although we hadn't any difficulty in agreeing, she was a cool, reserved sort of girl who came out of her room only at mealtimes. She'd insisted on having it arranged as a bed-sitter, and she spent all her time there—when she was at home, of course. I wasn't sorry when she left after only three months, and I tried for a time to manage on my own, but even though the rent was low, the expenses got too much for me. Then, just as

I was about to advertise again, your landlady gave you notice because she was selling up and going to live with her married daughter.' Hydee looked at her friend, and a lovely smile touched her lips, bringing an added glory to her eyes. 'You came to me, and it was the best thing that had happened to me since my father died.'

'And now I'll be leaving you on your own again.' Ellie swallowed hard, glanced at Hydee's empty plate and, rising rather abruptly, she picked up the two dinner plates and replaced them with the fruit sponge she had baked. 'I wish there was something I could do,' she sighed as she sat down again.

'Don't worry about me,' begged Hydee, distressed. 'I know I shall find the job I want.'

Ellie shook her head in swift and frowning protest. 'Living in can be exhausting. You need your time off, your leisure.'

'I'll certainly have time off,' stated Hydee with confidence. 'No one would expect me to be on duty for too long a stretch at a time. No, I intend to have my own private apartment in which I can relax when I'm off duty.'

'You seem to have it all cut and dried in your mind.' Ellie spoke more sharply than she intended, but her patience was frayed by her own helplessness. Hydee had encased herself in an armour of reserve immediately after she had been jilted, and that armour had remained in place ever since. She stayed in every night and on the weekends. True, Ellie had managed to get her to visit her own mother, and Ray's parents, but that was about as far as Hydee would go in being sociable. Ellie had tried to get Hydee to come on holiday with her and Ray, but Hydee had refused. Her excuse that she did not want to play gooseberry failed to deceive her friend. Hydee was still breaking her heart over Noel.

'I believe I do have it all cut and dried,' agreed Hydee, unconsciously breaking into her friend's thoughts. 'The only difficulty I can see is that of contacting someone who requires the help which I'm willing to give. I suppose some organisation like the Citizens' Advice Bureau could help.'

'Sounds a good bet, though I'm still of the opinion that you ought not to give up your home, Hydee.' There was a hint of persuasion in Ellie's voice as, after passing the jug of custard to her friend, she watched her pouring the creamy mixture over the fluffy confection on her plate.

'I might not be able to get a post where I live in, and in that case I won't be giving up my home.' Hydee spoke merely to ease Ellie's mind. For herself, she preferred to leave the flat now that Ellie was going away. The prospect of living entirely alone had recently become just as unacceptable as the idea of trying to find another compatible person to share the expenses, expenses which were still rising all the time so that, even if she had been willing to live alone, she would have found it difficult indeed to make ends meet.

'If you must have this new job,' Ellie said a short while later when they were sitting by the fire, drinking coffee and indulging in the luxury of the Grand Marnier liqueur which had been given to Ellie as a birthday present a couple of months ago, 'then I'd like to see things moving before I leave you.'

Hydee nodded, agreeing that she would certainly feel better if her future was settled by the time Ellie and Ray were married.

'I've a week's holiday to come shortly,' she went on, 'and I can spend it looking around.'

Ellie was silent, looking at her friend and wondering how any man could have jilted her. For she possessed a special beauty, with that young, almost childish face which had about it an ethereal quality that made it most arresting. There was certainly a subtle hint of mystery in the large brown eyes—an Oriental touch brought about by the slight uplift at the outer corners; there was an unmistakable charm in the high cheekbones, the clear alabaster skin, the delicate form of the mouth with its full, compassionate lips. The hair too was inordinately attractive, its colour an unusual blend of dark brown and russet, highlighted with strands of burnished copper. From the high, intelligent forehead it fell in gentle waves to Hydee's shoulders, flicking up into half curls at the ends.

Ellie sighed. If only Hydee would forget Noel, would shake off this aversion to men which stemmed from the fear of being jilted a second time, then she would very soon find someone to love her.

Chapter Two

As Hydee had said, she spent her holiday in looking around for the type of job on which she had set her heart. The various organisations she contacted were of little or no help; the advertisement she inserted in the newspaper did not bring the results which she had optimistically expected. She scanned the local papers and the nationals, and now, with only two days of her holiday left, she opened the *Times* with a dejected sigh, convinced there would be nothing to interest her.

But she was mistaken, and her eyes kindled with eagerness as she read the rather stiff and formal advertisement which must have been inserted at great cost, being a 'window' measuring three inches square.

'You've found something?' Ellie, who had been off work with a severe cold, was sitting by the fire, a book on her lap. 'If your expression's anything to go by, then you've seen something promising at last.'

Hydee nodded quickly and passed the newspaper to her friend, watching Ellie's expression change as she read and reread the ad, silently at first and then aloud.

' "Refined and cultured English lady required to take full charge of two children, a boy of seven and a girl of five. Must be prepared to live abroad. Reply by letter to: The Marquês Carlos de Alva Manrique, c/o the Dorchester Hotel, London." ' Ellie had read the advertisement slowly, saying the words with a sort of awed disbelief. 'Good heavens, Hydee,' she exclaimed in a more normal voice, 'you can't be thinking of answering an ad like that!'

'Why not? It sounds as if it might be just what I want. A home's being offered, which will suit me very well, and I must say that the idea of living abroad appeals to me.' She paused, her eyes more keenly bright than Ellie had ever seen them. 'You and Ray could come for your holidays.'

'Where to?' inquired her friend in a rather dry voice.

'Spain of course. The advertiser's Spanish, so it's reasonable to conclude that he lives in Spain.'

'He could be Portuguese,' Ellie pointed out. 'Would you like to live in Portugal?'

Hydee paused, eyes flickering. 'I think so. I've heard that it's a beautiful country.'

'So have I. However, I wouldn't bother about this advertisement if I were you. The man's name's enough to put one off. Marquês Carlos de Alva Manrique! Heavens, Hydee, you couldn't possibly get your tongue around all that every time you spoke to him!'

Hydee laughed. 'If he's Spanish, then he'll be called Don Carlos, and if he's Portuguese his title will be Dom.'

Ellie looked at her. 'Well, there's no doubt that you're eager, and as there's nothing to lose by answering the ad, go ahead.'

Hydee needed no encouragement; the letter was sent off that very morning. The reply came four days later, and the following Saturday afternoon Hydee was in the Dorchester Hotel, being shown up to the Crimson Suite which was occupied by the gentleman with the illustrious name, a tall, wide-shouldered man with a slender frame and all the marks of the aristocrat both in his finely chiselled face and in his regal bearing. He had already risen before she entered the sumptuous sitting room, and for a moment he stared at her; his penetrating eyes, dark as lignite but hard as steel, took in, in one swift appraisal, the whole of Hydee's appearance. She coloured, stirring uncomfortably. The marquês spoke at last in a low, cultured voice carrying a hint of accent which without doubt added to its attraction. Hydee felt small and insignificant and wondered what she was doing here at all, in this man's luxurious suite, waiting to see how she was to be treated.

'Please have a chair, Miss Merrill.' An immaculately kept hand, deceptively slender, motioned Hydee to a chair. 'And now,' he said when she was seated, 'perhaps you will tell me something about yourself.'

She looked questioningly at him, surprised that the interview should begin like this.

'What is it you want to know, sir?' There was a slight hesitation before the last word, because she was in doubt as to how she should address him. So proud he looked, with that aristocratic bearing and the self-confidence which comes naturally to those with a noble lineage.

'Perhaps,' he began formally, 'I should first instruct you as to the form of address I prefer. You are probably aware that in Portugal "Dom" is a title often used, along with the Christian name, for a Portuguese count, viscount, or marquis. You may address me as Dom Carlos or, more simply, as senhor.'

Hydee nodded her head. 'I understand,' she said.

The marquês sat down on a satin-covered sofa opposite her chair. 'And now,' he said again, 'you can tell me about yourself. You have obviously had experience with children. You took a course in child care, I suppose?'

Disconcerted, she gave a small start. 'No, I haven't, senhor,' she confessed, at which his eyes opened wide.

'What experience have you had, then?'

She bit her lip. What an idiot she had been to apply for the post when she had no experience to offer! She had blithely thought that her intense love of children would suffice. She still believed it would —but she could hardly expect the marquês to feel the same way about it.

'I have no experience whatsoever,' she admitted, her lovely eyes meeting his in a frank and honest stare.

For a moment there was silence in the room,

Hydee waiting dejectedly for the words of dismissal which she knew must come. But to her surprise the marquês said kindly, 'Why, Miss Merrill, have you applied for the post?'

With the same honest and unflinching stare, Hydee gave him her answer. 'I love children, sir— Dom Carlos—and I want to work with them. I did say in my letter that at present I'm working in an office; but for some time now I have been considering working with children.' Her voice, low-toned and musical, was as arresting as her words, and she saw that the marquês's interest was caught.

'True, you did say in your letter that you were working in an office, but I took it for granted that you'd had at least some experience with children. However, experience, though often desirable, is not always essential, especially in a post of this kind. . . .' He allowed his voice to trail off obscurely, just as if, thought Hydee, there was something not quite orthodox about the post he was offering. 'Senhorita, do you sincerely love children?'

'Yes,' she answered simply, 'I do, and that's the reason why I want to work with them.' She paused a moment, then said, 'If you would give me a trial, senhor, I am sure you would be more than satisfied with me.' The low tones had taken on a note of unconscious pleading and the large brown eyes had a limpid quality that seemed to tell the man watching her that tears of sadness often lingered within their depths.

'Are your children here with you?' ventured Hydee when he remained silent. 'If . . . if they and I could meet . . . ?' She stopped as he shook his head.

'I omitted to mention in my letter that my son and

daughter are at present staying in Surrey with a friend of my late wife. . . .' Again his voice trailed off, and this time the fine mouth went tight, the noble jaw flexed. With her quick intelligence, Hydee immediately sensed anger and contempt mingling to form the harsh expression which now marred the good looks which had been the first thing to strike her about the marquês. 'The confinement of a hotel is not good for boisterous children like mine,' he added, and now a smile appeared, erasing the displeasure of a moment earlier.

'They're boisterous?' Hydee's voice held surprise. 'I wouldn't have expected them . . . ' She broke off, colouring at the thought of what she had been about to say. The marquês finished the sentence for her, saying that she would not have expected the children of a Portuguese nobleman to be boisterous but, rather, to have their high spirits suppressed by dignity.

'My children, senhorita,' he continued, his face unsmiling but amusement clearly portrayed in his voice, 'are in no way inhibited by convention. For the past two years they have known what freedom is.' He paused, deep in thought. What about the past? wondered Hydee. The past *beyond* two years ago. She knew instinctively that his wife had been dead for two years; she also felt fairly sure that up till then the children had been far more restricted than they were now. She continued to watch the marquês's thoughtful face. He seemed almost to have forgotten about the interview he was conducting and, after several more silent moments, she gave a little cough which immediately brought him back. He put more questions to her, learning that she had no parents—no relations whatsoever—that she was sharing a flat with a friend who would shortly be leaving to get married. He probably learned as much from what was left unsaid, thought Hydee, noting his expression as it changed from time to time.

'So you're totally alone in the world?' The dark eyes were fixed intently upon her; she turned her head a little, disconcerted by his stare. 'When this friend leaves you, you'll have no one at all?'

She shook her head, unhappily aware that he must be wondering why she had no other friends, and perhaps he was concluding that the fault lay in some aspect of her personality. Like any other person, Hydee hated anyone to think that she was disliked and, accordingly, words rose to her lips that would otherwise never have been voiced. 'My lack of friends, senhor, is a product of my own desire. I prefer solitude.'

'You prefer solitude?' The marquês raised his eyebrows. 'You'll not find much solitude in looking after children.'

'No. . . .' She knew she had made a mistake, but there was little she could do about it. 'Children are different,' she murmured, convinced that the interview was not going in her favour.

To her surprise, he bypassed this remark, asking her more about herself and her late parents. After three or four minutes he said, 'Miss Merrill, I'm impressed by all you have told me, and the next thing is for you to meet my children. Can you get time off from work?'

'Yes, if it's necessary. I haven't told my employer that I'm looking for another post, but I'm sure he'll understand when I do tell him, and he'll let me have a day off.' She was slightly breathless, the result of excitement. Was the post really hers? It would seem so, and she marvelled that she had managed to impress the aristocratic Marquês Carlos de Alva Manrique, impress him with nothing more than the honest summary of her life history. Of course, the securing of the post ultimately depended on whether she and the children got along together, but in her present state of optimism Hydee envisaged no snags whatever. Always she'd had a way with children, especially young ones, and she had no qualms about the forthcoming meeting with the two, who, she hoped, would soon be given into her charge.

'You will need to ask for more than one day, senhorita. I should like you to stay with my children —whose names, by the way, are Ramos and Luisa— for a few days at least. I must make sure this time. . . .' He broke off, frowning. The idea that he could be unsure what to say made him seem more human, less exalted than before.

'You've had some difficulty with your nannies, senhor?' she ventured.

He nodded, the frown deepening. 'Considerable difficulty, Miss Merrill.' Brusque the voice now, giving Hydee her first fleeting tinge of anxiety. Was the marquês so hard to please that no nanny had been able to tolerate his interference regarding the children? 'So much difficulty that I have changed my plans for the children's future—' He raised an imperious hand to dismiss the interruption which came to Hydee's lips. 'This will not concern you at this stage, senhorita. Meet my children first, and then we can talk of other things.'

Chapter Three

'Other things,' murmured Ellie, puzzled. 'What did he mean?'

'I have no idea, but he certainly sounded mysterious.' Hydee and Ellie were eating their evening meal, Hydee having arrived home from her trip to London in plenty of time to prepare it before Ellie came in from the office. As soon as they sat down, she had begun to relate what had transpired at the interview, ending up just as the marquês had done, by mentioning those 'other things.'

'If you ask me,' offered Ellie, 'there's more to this job than appears on the surface.'

'But in what way?' Hydee frowned, wishing she could shake off this tinge of uneasiness concerning the post which she so desperately wanted to obtain. She had set her heart on it. In fact, she'd been unable to think of anything else as she sat in the train coming up from London. Nanny to the children of a marquês! Of course *any* children would have done, but she was honest enough to admit that the idea of working for such an exalted man held certain attractions, as did the prospect of living in Portugal in what must surely be a mansion, even if only a small one. 'I've racked my brain to find an explanation, but I can't.'

'He's had trouble with his previous nannies, you said?'

'Yes. The actual words he used were "considerable difficulty."'

'How many nannies has he had altogether in these two years he mentioned?'

'He didn't say, but I had the impression that he's had several.'

'Because of what he said about making sure this time?'

Hydee nodded, trying to throw out the idea that all was not aboveboard, but failing to do so because her logical mind insisted on warning her of a snag.

'Yes,' she answered, glancing across the table at Ellie. 'It's because of these troubles he's had that he insists I stay with the children for a few days.'

'Seems phony to me!'

'It isn't phony,' Hydee was swift to contradict. 'The marquês is cold and aloof, but his integrity's not to be questioned.'

'He certainly made a favourable impression on *you*.' Ellie's voice was dry and left Hydee with no illusions regarding her friend's disapproval. Ellie had not even wanted Hydee to attend the interview, declaring the marquês's letter to be far too stiff and formal; he would certainly not be a kind, understanding man and, therefore, would obviously be a difficult employer.

'He did indeed,' Hydee's tone was reflective. 'He could have told me to leave once he knew I had no qualifications, but, on the contrary, he wanted to know more about me.'

'Too darned much, if you ask me,' returned Ellie darkly. 'Why on earth should he want to know about your parents? Why was he so interested in the fact that you had no relatives? You shouldn't have been so keen to reveal it to him,' added Ellie severely. 'I'm sure I wouldn't have answered all those questions!'

'It's not unnatural that he should want to learn a little of my background,' protested Hydee in defence of the marquês. 'I haven't any recommendations, remember, so he has to do something to make sure I'm genuine.'

'He's only to look at you to see that!'

'He isn't you,' laughed Hydee. 'He's never met me before; he knows nothing about me—'

'He knows just about everything, if you ask me!'

'You know what I mean,' said Hydee patiently. 'Just put yourself in his place for a moment. He's thinking of employing me to look after his two young children. It's not unreasonable that he should want to know as much about me as he possibly can.'

A deep sigh was Ellie's only answer as she toyed absently with the mixed vegetables on her plate, going over in her mind all that Hydee had told her.

'I don't like the sound of it,' she said stubbornly at length. 'Take my advice, Hydee, and let the matter rest where it is.'

'I can't do a thing like that! He's expecting me to telephone him and say when I can go down to Surrey.'

'Why does he need an English nanny anyway?' pursued Ellie, just as if Hydee had not spoken at all. 'Were those other nannies English?'

'I can't say. And as to why he wants an English nanny this time—well, he did mention that his children speak our language.'

'What does that signify? Most foreign kids are taught English as their second language.'

'I expect he'll explain eventually,' said Hydee.

'If I were you, I'd telephone him this very evening and tell him the whole thing's off. It's far too risky, going over there to his home.' Ellie shook her head emphatically. 'You mustn't do it, Hydee!'

'I'm sorry you're so troubled, Ellie, and it's certainly gratifying to know that there's at least one person in the world who cares what's to become of me. However, I am old enough to take care of myself, but in any case, we're travelling a little too fast. I haven't landed the job yet. The children might not take to me—'

'You know darned well they'll take to you,' interrupted her friend impatiently. 'All kids take to you!'

Hydee had to smile at Ellie's anger. Yet, as she had just remarked, it was gratifying to know that there was someone who really cared. It meant a great deal to Hydee to know that if she did take this post abroad, she would at least have a contact with home, for she was sure that she and Ellie would keep up a regular correspondence with one another.

'I want to go to Surrey,' she said at length, almost apologetically. 'Please bear with me, Ellie, as I'm really anxious to take the job if it's offered to me.'

'In spite of the mystery?'

'There won't be a mystery after I've been to Surrey. The marquês did say, remember, that we'd talk about these other things. It's my opinion that he intends to make some alterations in the way he wants the children brought up.'

Ellie's eyes flickered thoughtfully, and when she spoke, her voice was not as sharp as before. 'That would certainly explain what he said about those "other things" which have been worrying us. In fact, he said he had changed his plans for the children's future, didn't he?'

'Yes, that's right.' Hydee was glad that Ellie seemed a little less hostile towards the marquês, and she hoped to be able to tell her, on her return from Surrey, that everything had been satisfactorily explained and that all her suspicions were unfounded.

The house in Surrey was far less pretentious than Hydee had expected. It was of a moderate size with no more than an acre of garden surrounding it and a small paddock to one side. The marquês, who had met Hydee at the station in a chauffeur-driven car which bore a silver crest on each of its four doors and flew a pennant above the windscreen, had spoken very little to Hydee after the first rather cool greeting as he met her on the platform, and she was now experiencing a sort of weighty sensation in the pit of her stomach. The marquês's strange mood affected her in an uncomfortable manner and she even dwelt on the possibility of his having regretted asking her to come to Surrey to meet his children. Perhaps he had now decided he ought to look for a woman with experience. Undoubtedly there were plenty to be had, women whose careers had started with a two-

or three-year course in child care, followed by experience gained in the sort of post for which they had trained.

'Well, here we are,' the marquês said as the big car turned into the short but well-kept drive. 'You'll be meeting the children, but they have no idea who you are.'

She nodded. 'I understand,' she said, smiling.

The chauffeur, whom the marquês called Casco, opened the door for Hydee to alight, then went round the car to do the same for the marquês. Within a few minutes Hydee had met Mrs. Doreen Fitzwarren, who at present had charge of the children.

A tall, attractive woman of about thirty, she instantly put Hydee at her ease by saying, after the introduction had been made, 'Carlos was telling me on the phone that you come from Crady-on-Sea. I used to live there myself when I was in my teens. I expect it's changed since I left more than twelve years ago.'

'It hasn't changed very much. There are a few more hotels, of course, to deal with the extra holidaymakers who've recently been attracted to the resort.' Her thoughts went quite naturally to Noel, who, as manager of the White Hart, had brought about a threefold increase in profits, gaining promotion for himself as a result.

Doreen began speaking to the marquês rather quietly, and Hydee, undecided as to whether or not she was meant to overhear, moved towards the open window, where she caught her first glimpse of the children. Ramos and Luisa. . . . Both dark like their father, both extraordinarily good-looking, Ramos in a strong, classical way, with a firm chin even now,

and the same jawline as his father. Hydee could not
see his eyes but knew instinctively that they were
dark brown. Luisa's prettiness was equally marked,
but in a more gentle way. Her delicate little face,
with its pointed chin and rosebud mouth, was
creased with laughter now as she stood before her
brother, who, having come into contact with something sharp, was looking with dismay at the large
tear in his denim shorts. Hydee's mouth curved and
her eyes lit with amusement. They were *natural*, at
any rate, just as she had hoped they would be. For
she had come with some slight doubts in spite of
their father's assertion that they were in no way
inhibited by convention.

She was still smiling in amusement when, ad-
dressed by the marquês, she turned round to face
him. She saw his eyes flicker, then move slowly to
the scene outside, where his daughter was still
laughing and his son just about to give her something
which would take the humour from her face. This he
did, but playfully, and then they were sparring
together; they fell into a flower border, where the
struggle continued.

Ramos cried, 'Stop biting me!' in English, and his
sister returned, 'Then you stop punching *me!* If
you're not careful, you'll tear your silly old pants
even more—and that'll be funnier than ever because
it'll show your—'

'Luisa! Ramos!' Their father's voice brought the
children instantly to their feet. 'That's enough.
Come here and meet a friend of mine.'

Hydee looked swiftly at him, the colour rising to
tint her cheeks. So naturally he had referred to her
as his friend, yet it was as a servant that she was
entering his employ. Her thoughts faded as a wry

31

expression crossed her face. She was taking far too much for granted. She might be a little more then halfway to obtaining the post, but the biggest hurdle had yet to be surmounted.

Would these lovely children like her? she wondered, apprehension suddenly filling her heart.

'I'll go and leave you to it, Carlos,' Doreen said, her glance darting to the French window, which was partly open, and through which the children would come racing in a few seconds. 'You'll be staying for dinner, I hope?' And she was gone without waiting for an answer from the marquês.

'Papa!' Both children spoke together. 'You've been gone a long time! Where have you been?' Ramos wanted to know, the words interspersed with great gulps of air. 'We want to go home!'

Hydee, a little surprised that they seemed to speak English all the time, looked at the marquês inquiringly.

'Their mother was English,' he explained without much expression. 'Ramos, Luisa, meet Miss Merrill. She will be staying here with you for a few days.'

'Oh. . . .' Both children subjected Hydee to. a long and disconcerting scrutiny before Ramos said respectfully, 'How do you do, Miss Merrill?'

She smiled, took the hand extended to her, and knew that she and the boy were going to be friends. Luisa, however, was more undecided, her wide hazel eyes fixed on Hydee's face as if she were unable to take them from it. The moment was tense, with Hydee aware of what lay in the balance. Standing immobile, the marquês watched his daughter intently through partly narrowed eyes.

'Say how do you do to Miss Merrill,' he ordered

when eventually the silence stretched to the point where Hydee was plainly becoming uncomfortable.

'How do you do . . . Miss Merrill?' A small hand was outstretched obediently. Hydee took it and found it to be cold. This, and the child's long hesitation, convinced her that the post was lost.

She looked unhappily at the marquês who, after telling the children to go out again into the garden, turned to her with a kindly smile and said, much to her surprise, 'It would seem that Ramos has taken to you, senhorita. Luisa has always been more reserved in her manner, but she will come round eventually.'

'You mean,' faltered Hydee, stunned, 'that you are willing to engage me as nanny to your children?'

A silence followed, unfathomable and profound. And when presently the marquês spoke, her question had been ignored. 'For the present, Miss Merrill, it will be enough that you become used to the children, and they to you. Tomorrow morning I must leave for London, as I have business to conduct there. I shall return here on Saturday and stay with you and the children over the weekend.' That was all; his tone had changed, a quality entering it that was final and implacable. The lordly Marquês Carlos de Alva Manrique did not intend to be questioned, even though he must be aware of Hydee's bewilderment. She bit her lip in vexation, feeling cheated—snubbed, even—and the merest hint of anger rose within her. However, she had no difficulty in hiding it, and for the next few minutes she and the Marquês chatted amicably enough, with Hydee answering several personal questions he asked but avoiding the delicate matter of her broken engagement.

He had expressed what seemed to be sincere

regret that she was alone in the world, but Hydee felt he was not really sorry for her loss—on the contrary, she sensed that he was glad she had no one of her own. She naturally allowed her thoughts to stray to what Ellie had said, and to recall vividly her suspicions. Well, it would seem that any explanation of the mystery must wait until the weekend, when the marquês returned to Surrey.

Chapter Four

The next few days passed quickly, and before she quite knew it, Hydee was eagerly looking forward to the following day—Saturday—when the marquês would be returning to the house of his late wife's friend. During the time she had been staying in Doreen's home, Hydee had learned a good deal about the marquês, but little about his late wife. For it had been clear right from the start that Doreen was reluctant to talk about her friend and, therefore, Hydee had refrained from putting questions to her. Hydee was not so obliging when it came to the subject of the nannies which the children had had in the past, though. Doreen, being ready to enlighten Hydee, told her about the first one, who was Portuguese.

'She fell in love with Carlos almost immediately. It was so absurd, as she knew that Eunice had been dead less than a month.'

'The marquês—he'd be furious, naturally?'

Doreen nodded. 'He soon sent her packing. The next one was also Portuguese, coming from a well-to-do family who'd come into hard times. But she hadn't lost any of her arrogance, it seemed. I was over at the Palacio de Manrique—I went for a holiday just after my divorce came through,' she went on to explain, straying from what she had been going to say. 'I was feeling low at the time, even though the decision to separate was mutual. We couldn't get along and so we decided to make the break before we started to hate each other. Sensible, don't you think?'

'I suppose so,' replied Hydee reluctantly.

'You don't believe in divorce, obviously?'

'I do, yes. It's the only answer when two people can't get along. But it's so sad. . . .' For a moment Hydee thought of Noel, and how he and she used to say that no matter what others did, no matter how many of their friends and acquaintances might part, they would be together until the very end of their lives, for they would live in a realm where no storms came. He was going to become an integral part of her life, and from the time of their engagement Hydee had begun to think in twos. No matter what she considered, the thought that Noel would either like this thing or not was never far from her mind and governed everything she did. When he had come to her to say it was all over between them, Hydee had had no idea of what she was going to do without him. What did others do? she wondered. Let time fill the gaps, wait for memory to lose its

36

sharp outlines and die away? 'Yes, it's sad,' went on Hydee at length. 'After all, every married couple begins by being in love.'

The older woman nodded, but said with a hint of humour, 'Except in marriages of convenience. One hears of them but never meets the people involved. Do they really happen, I wonder?'

Hydee shook her head. 'I shouldn't think so,' she said. And, after only a slight pause, 'You were telling me about the nannies who've been employed by the marquês.'

'Yes. I ought to tell you as much as I can, so that you won't make the same mistakes they did.' She went on, repeating that she had met the second of the nannies when she was on holiday at the marquês's home; the girl obviously resented the fact that she was forced to work for a living, and she also forgot that she was there in the role of nanny and not as mistress of the establishment. Carlos soon became plagued with complaints from his staff that Rosinha was issuing orders to the servants. And reluctant as he was to dismiss her—having known her brother since they were both at college—Carlos did finally send her the way of the first one. Doreen continued for some minutes; Hydee counted five nannies in all. 'It's not good for the children, and they've run a little wild lately, although they don't seem to have lost anything by that.'

'The marquês seems to favour freedom for his children.'

'He does to a great extent believe in freedom, but he can be exceptionally stern if either Ramos or Luisa is really naughty.'

'Why has he suddenly decided to have an English nanny?' Hydee asked eventually.

'That's something I can't explain,' admitted Doreen. 'I haven't asked Carlos because, good friends though we are, he has never been really confiding. He's an aloof man and often unfathomable. His pride seems to prevent him from lowering his reserve too much—but perhaps you yourself have noticed how unapproachable he is?'

'I haven't seen enough of him to have formed an opinion,' returned Hydee in a guarded tone. 'But I agree with you that he's unfathomable.' She was thinking of the 'mystery' of which she and Ellie had spoken, and hoped that tomorrow would see it solved to her satisfaction. The disappointment would be unbearable if something should prevent her from obtaining the post. Ramos had taken to her from the first, and even though Luisa was still shy and distant, Hydee had noticed a slight change in the little girl during the past few days. She would now join in the games which Hydee played with Ramos, and she listened with interest when Hydee read stories from a book she had bought one afternoon when she and Doreen took the children for a car ride and a picnic in the woods.

Doreen had told Hydee about the Palacio and the splendour of its furnishings; she had also mentioned the marquês's numerous interests: his vineyards, his cork-oak forests, his several estates—*quintas*—of which the Quinta de Manrique was by far the largest.

'And now,' Doreen was saying as she and Hydee dined together on Friday evening, 'you know just about everything you need to know of your future employer.'

Hydee's eyes lit up. 'You really believe I'll get the post, then?'

38

'I'm sure of it. Carlos had a long conversation with me over the telephone, and it was plain that he was satisfied with you and what you had to offer—'

'I have nothing in the way of experience,' broke in Hydee, just because she had to. 'I shall always marvel that I even got a hearing!'

'He's a strange man.' Doreen nodded musingly. 'If he were engaging a butler or a housekeeper, he'd not even look at one who had no qualifications, yet over this nanny business—and with you especially —he seems to attach far more inportance to personality. I was amazed when he said you'd no experience, but of course I made no comment. It wasn't for me to voice an opinion—which he would have ignored anyway,' she added with a grimace. Hydee said nothing, as she was concentrating on her food, and after a moment Doreen spoke again. 'I've said you know just about everything you need to know about Carlos, but I feel that perhaps I ought to warn you of the young woman who has recently come to have designs on him. She's Portuguese and her name's Arminda Venancio. She and her mother have taken a rather pretty villa about three miles from the Palacio and Carlos has become friendly with her, from what I can gather. However, I have a friend living fairly close to the Venancio residence and she maintains that Arminda's a really nasty type beneath the façade she puts on for people like the marquês.'

'Surely the marquês would be able to see through her?'

'I'd have thought so myself,' agreed Doreen, but went on to add that even a man like the marquês was not always strongly enough armoured against

39

women whose attractions and charm were as potent as that of the beautiful Portuguese girl. 'She's obviously interested in his title and his wealth,' continued Doreen casually, 'and this friend of mine declares that it'll be a miracle if he remains single much longer.'

Hydee fell silent, a sort of chill settling on her. She could not have found a reason for it no matter how she tried, as it was far from logical to suppose that the existence of a girlfriend in her employer's life would affect her in any way at all.

The following morning dawned bright and sunny, and Hydee was on the lawn with the children when, at half-past eleven, the big limousine turned into the gateway and drew up at the end of the drive. Hydee watched as the children, having abandoned the game as soon as they saw the car, raced across the grass and literally flung themselves at their father. He caught them, one hanging on either arm, and swung them off their feet. Laughing, they asked for more, but the marquês told them to run along and play, as he wished to talk with Miss Merrill. They obeyed at once, and as Doreen was out, having gone to do some shopping, the time was most opportune. Hydee and the marquês went into the living room and sat down. Without any hesitation Dom Carlos admitted that he had asked Doreen to stay in constant touch with him by telephone, keeping him informed as to the relationship developing between Hydee and his two children.

'It's obvious to me that you have an excellent rapport with Ramos already, and that Luisa is gradually coming round.' The marquês spoke formally, but kindly for all that. Yet his thoughts seemed far away, as if what he really wanted to say had to be brought from some remote part of his mind. 'I take it, senhorita, that you are willing to care for my children?'

Hydee's heart jerked, then began to beat almost suffocatingly. The post was hers! She had been fairly certain, but only now was she *sure*.

'Yes, indeed, senhor,' she managed, although not in her usual calm and steady tone of voice. 'It will make me very happy to take up the position of nanny to Ramos and Luisa.'

A silence fell, deep and profound. The marquês stared at her speculatively before he said, slowly and deliberately, 'I am not looking for a nanny, Miss Merrill.'

'Not . . . ?' She blinked at him, uncertain whether she had heard correctly. 'What did you say, Dom Carlos?'

'I am not looking for a nanny.'

'But . . .' Hydee shook her head in bewilderment. What was wrong with him? He just asked if she were willing to care for his children, and now he was calmly informing her that he didn't want a nanny! 'I'm afraid I don't understand you, senhor.'

The trace of a smile touched the fine outline of his mouth. 'My children have had five nannies in two years,' he said. 'Nannies are obviously unsatisfactory, not the answer in this particular case. Miss Merrill, Ramos and Luisa need a mother.' His dark eyes, holding hers, seemed to have lost much of their hardness, and a little of their arrogance as well. 'I am looking for a wife, senhorita, and I feel sure that you, in your present situation, would be better for having a husband—' He stopped as Hydee gave a smothered exclamation, and then went on. 'You'd

41

no longer be alone in the world; you'd have the care and company of the children, which is what you want. I believe you will like my home, and be happy in it. Security will be yours—'

'Senhor!' broke in Hydee with a feeble lift of her hand. 'Please don't go on. This suggestion's preposterous! We scarcely know one another.' She was on the point of tears, so great was the disappointment flooding over her. 'Oh, please, sir,' she cried in tones of desperate pleading, 'let me be their nanny! I promise I'll do everything for them, be like a mother if that is what you want. Please, senhor. . . .'

He shook his head, and she saw the firm, implacable line of his jaw. 'Think about it, senhorita,' he advised. 'The proposition naturally comes as a shock to you, and your reaction is understandable. However, you will think more rationally when you've allowed yourself time to take in what I've said. I shall be here, with you and the children, for the weekend. I arranged it this way so that we can all be together as a family—'

'No!' Hydee broke in again, anger rising as a result of her bitter disappointment. 'I can't marry you!'

'Can you give me one good reason for making so vehement a declaration?' inquired the marquês in his quiet foreign voice.

Hydee shook her head, unable to think clearly, conscious of the weight of misery pressing down upon her.

'It . . . it w-wasn't f-fair of you to . . . to let me be w-with them like I have. . . .' Hydee stopped, the words blocked by the sob in her throat. 'We've g-got to like each other—especially Ramos—he's g-going to m-miss me. . . .' Again she stopped, aware that her stammered words might be incoherent but caring nothing for that. And she went on before Dom Carlos could insert any comments of his own, 'Ramos guessed that I was to . . . to be his new n-nanny, and he was happy about it. Luisa w-was c-coming round, as you s-said, and now it's all over. . . .'

Hydee's voice failed completely; she turned from the marquês, put her face in her hands and wept bitterly into them. For a long moment she was allowed the slight relief of her tears, and then, before she was aware of what was happening, she felt a strong arm about her shoulders, knew the comfort of a gentle hand on her hot forehead, heard the marquês's soft and understanding voice declaring that it was *not* all over, that she must calm herself and, having done so, she must sit quietly on her own and consider the advantages of accepting his proposal of marriage.

For a space she looked up at him through her tears, and then, much to her amazement, she heard herself say, 'Very well, Dom Carlos, I'll do as you advise.'

Ellie, her face pale with concern, looked at her friend and said, for what seemed the fiftieth time, 'You can't do it! The man's a stranger to you! In addition he's a foreigner, with a totally different temperament from yours. His way of life would soon become irksome, what with its restrictions, its narrow confines, which preclude the freedom you've been used to! And what of his position? You'd be like a fish out of water in this Palacio you've mentioned! I'm not being critical, Hydee, just honest; I want to make you see reason.' She stopped at last and Hydee gave a small sigh of relief. She and Ellie

43

had been through this many times during the last two days, but Hydee had retained her patience, fully appreciative of the fact that her friend's attempts to dissuade her from marrying the marquês were made with the very best of intentions. Ellie truly believed that Hydee was making a mistake, that in no time at all she would be regretting what, in Ellie's words, was 'an impulsive, idiotic action inspired by your obsession to be with children.'

'I want to marry him,' murmured Hydee at last, speaking over her shoulder, for she had moved to the window and was looking out to the garden, where a group of small children played on the grass. They were from the adjoining flats, and the mother of one of them was watching to make sure they came to no harm. 'I've been given the opportunity of becoming a wife and a mother, and I'd be a fool to turn it down— No, please don't interrupt,' she said quickly on hearing Ellie's impatient exclamation. 'I want to make you understand. Carlos is a good man who'll keep to his promise. It will be a marriage of convenience, no matter what you've said to the contrary. You seem convinced that he'll . . . he'll . . .' Hydee broke off, colouring with embarrassment.

Her friend said, uncaring for her feelings on the matter, 'He'll take you when the urge gets him, and don't you kid yourself that he won't! Man of honour or not he's got the same primitive instincts as any other healthy male, and he isn't going to have qualms about asserting his rights—'

'Don't, Ellie, please! I hate this kind of talk!'

'Inhibitions, because of your determination not to be a proper wife—because of what you still feel for

Noel. Hydee, for heaven's sake put the silly notion
of marrying this foreign marquês out of your head!'

'I can't. I've made a promise and I'm going to
keep it. As I've told you, Ramos likes me and his
sister won't be long in accepting me. In fact, she's
not nearly so shy and reserved now as she was at
first.'

'By "now" I take it that you mean last weekend.
You haven't seen these children for two days, and I'd
not be in the least surprised if they've forgotten you
already.'

'Well, they'll soon get used to me again. After
Saturday I shall be with them all the time.'

'Saturday . . .' A heavy frown settled on Ellie's
forehead. 'He didn't give you much time, did he?'

'He gave me what I asked for. I'd rather get it over
and done with, and settle into my new way of life.'

' "Get it over and done with," ' seethed Ellie, still
trying to convince her friend of the error she was
making. 'What a way to talk about one's wedding
day!'

Hydee coloured, cursing herself for that slip of the
tongue. She ought to have known Ellie would seize
on it and deliver some disparaging remark.

'The wedding's a mere formality,' she reminded
her. 'I shall be in the position of nanny, really.'

'Wife in name only, with the position of nanny!
You must be out of your mind!' Ellie looked at her
squarely and went on in tones of dark foreboding,
'You'll regret this madness before you're a month
older!'

Hydee had to smile. It was surprising, she had to
admit, how optimistic she was about the step she had
decided to take.

'I expect we'll survive for longer than that,' she stated. 'The children are Carlos's first concern, and therefore he isn't going to do anything that will upset me. Surely you can see that?'

'The only thing I can see is disaster!'

'And I can see only a very pleasant, happy and contented existence.'

'You'll be contented with no love in your life?'

'The children will love me. I shall do everything in my power to make them love me.'

'So confident! A normally sensible girl going like a lamb to the slaughter!'

'Ellie,' said Hydee persuasively after a pause, 'don't go on any more, please. I know I'm making the right decision.'

'If only you could forget Noel. . . .' Ellie allowed her voice to trail away to silence, the expression on her face one of anger mingled with resignation. 'I give in,' she almost snapped. 'Yes, Hydee, I give in.'

And once having come to accept that Hydee's mind was firmly made up, Ellie successfully hid her misgivings and helped Hydee all she could to settle her affairs. There were things to sell, some of which Ellie bought for the home she and Ray were setting up. Other, more personal possessions were carefully packed in the crate which Carlos had had sent to the flat by a firm of movers who would themselves have done the packing, but Hydee preferred to do it herself in her own time. The crate was then collected by the shippers, who would see that it arrived safely at the Palacio. Hydee had explained to her employer that she was getting married the following Saturday and going to live abroad. If he experienced any astonishment, he hid it, and as he'd had a young lady in mind for a job for some time, he obligingly allowed Hydee to leave on Wednesday afternoon, as this other young lady was ready to start work on Thursday morning.

On Saturday Hydee and the marquês were married by special licence in the little church not far from the bridge on which she had so often stood, looking from the hills to the sea and then staring at the river beneath her, watching its sparkling waters flowing towards the wide blue ocean. She was in a charming suit of beige linen with coffee-coloured embroidery on the lapels of the jacket. Her handbag, shoes and gloves matched the embroidery, but her hat was of the same shade as the suit. Ellie and Ray were there, and that was all. It was a very quiet wedding; no emotion, no glances of love between the bridegroom and his bride, no kiss, no confetti. . . .

And less than two hours after the ceremony Hydee—the Marquesa de Alva Manrique—was boarding an airplane with her husband, the children having been taken to Portugal two days previously by Doreen. Lunch was served on the plane, but Hydee could not eat. What had she done? Carried along as she had been by the unveering desire to have a post where she could be with children, she had had no time for anything other than those numerous, all-absorbing tasks that would bring her nearer to her goal. But now . . .

Chapter Five

During the flight Hydee had several times attempted
to engage her husband in conversation, but for the
most part he was silent and she became acutely
conscious of his withdrawal. She fell to wondering if
he were recalling his first marriage and the occasion
of his bringing another English bride to his ancestral
home in one of the most beautiful regions of Portugal. On that occasion he was in love, though, with a
woman who loved him. Now there was no love on
either side; it was purely and simply a marriage of
convenience which would never have taken place but
for the needs of his two young children.

A small sigh escaped her, and inevitably her mind
turned to those idyllic days of her engagement to

Noel. It was on a sparkling winter afternoon, when they were both part of a skating party on a lake, that they had first met, having tumbled after colliding with one another. Their laughter had echoed on the crystal air; they had dined together that evening, and that was how it all began.

Hydee, with a mental shake, thrust the memories from her mind and dwelt instead on the few things she had learned about her husband, mainly from Doreen, but a little from Carlos himself. She knew he had no parents but did have a sister, Isobella, two years younger than he, married with one young son, Pedro, aged seven, the same age as Ramos. She knew he had several aunts and uncles, and two cousins, Gasper, a bachelor, and Ines, married only a few months ago. All these people descended on the Palacio for the Christmas celebrations and stayed on for several days. Hydee had also learned a little about the business of wine-making—the collection of the ripe grapes in large baskets and their transportation to the *adegas*, where they were trod, sieved, and the juice left to ferment.

'You will enjoy the vintage,' Doreen had said, for there was much fun and merrymaking after all the hard work was over and the harvesting done.

'You're a long way off, Hydee.' Carlos's quiet voice broke into Hydee's musings, and she smiled at him, nodding her head.

'I was thinking of what Doreen said about the vintage. I shall look forward to it.'

'It'll be starting in September. Then, after that, our next festivity's Christmas.' He went on to explain how different it was from an English Christmas, and as he continued to speak, Hydee had the impression that he had decided he'd neglected her too long and was feeling a trifle guilty because of it. Perhaps he was sorry for her, too, and a little concerned, aware that she must be feeling rather lost and lonely, coming like this to a foreign land, with a man she scarcely knew.

'Christmas sounds fascinating,' she commented when he had stopped speaking. 'Just think, it's only about four months away.'

'Time passes swiftly.' He took up the airline's complimentary magazine and idly thumbed the pages. So once again Hydee was left to her own thoughts, and they turned to the children, who for a full week were staying with their Aunt Isobella at her mansion, which was situated four miles from the Palacio. Carlos had said he was doing this so that Hydee could settle in before assuming her duties; she must get to know her way about, must become familiar with the servants.

'They all speak English tolerably well,' he had told her, so she would have no trouble being understood.

'All?' she had faltered, this being another aspect of her new life which she had not examined. 'How . . . how many are there?'

'A large number. You'll meet some of them as soon as we arrive at the Palacio.' He had already sent word that he was married and that the servants would be expected to be there, ready to meet his wife.

On hearing this, Hydee was filled with consternation, visualising a long line of servants standing there in respectful silence, waiting in a state of extreme curiosity to meet the new marquesa.

'It will be too overwhelming,' she had said, an unconscious plea in her voice. 'Couldn't I meet them one at a time?'

He had laughed then and informed her that it would be impossible for her to meet them all, anyway.

'There are hundreds of workers on the estate. You will meet the house servants only, the ones with whom you'll be coming into daily contact. The rest will meet you later.'

'I see. Thank you,' she murmured, and again he seemed amused.

Hydee looked out the window, seeing only clouds. They were still very high, but she guessed they were not too far from their destination. Casting a sideways glance at her husband, seeing the forbidding line of his profile, she knew again a sense of misgiving, and another little sigh escaped her, this time to be heard, bringing Carlos's head round in a gesture of inquiry.

When she did not speak, he asked if anything were wrong. 'You look depressed,' he observed, frowning.

Depressed, on her wedding day. Yes, it was the truth, and yet alongside her depression was the determination to make something of her life now that the opportunity had been given her.

'I suppose it's apprehension,' she confessed, an unconscious little catch in her voice that made her seem very young, like a child, almost. 'The dramatic change in my life-style, for one thing, and the change of occupation, too. . . .' She stopped, because his straight black eyebrows had risen, and because of the look of censure that was darkening his eyes. 'I feel I'm nothing more than a nanny,' she said by way of explanation.

'You're my wife,' he returned softly and, to Hydee's ears, a little warningly. 'I shall expect you to act normally, as a wife would be expected to act, around the servants. I abhor gossip in the kitchen, and unless you remember your position as the Marquesa de Alva Manrique, there will certainly be gossip.'

Warmth came to her cheeks, mantling them with colour. How could she possibly assume the dignity which her husband obviously expected of her when she had no experience of the life to which he was used?

'I'm sorry,' was all she could find to say, and she fully expected him to leave her to her own reflections yet again. But instead he made polite conversation, for which she was grateful, as it brought her out of her dejection. At last the sound of the engines changed and the plane began its descent. A little while later it made a smooth landing on the broad runway and then turned and slowed before taxiing to a stop. Within half an hour Hydee, her husband's hand lightly beneath her elbow, was moving towards a sleek white limousine. She noticed the immaculate uniformed chauffeur waiting, the silver crest above the car's radiator, the arms emblazoned on the panel of each door. How many cars and chauffeurs did Carlos have? she wondered, realising that the car he had used in London must be coming back by ship, along with Casco. Dazed by all that was happening to her, she afterwards realised that she scarcely took in much at all until they were speeding smoothly along the road and she was leaning back, relaxed, against the soft luxury of the upholstery. She glanced at Carlos, at the forbidding profile, haughty and noble, familiar by now in its bronzed impressiveness. She moved her glance to the window, and her heart was lighter all at once, for all this was novel

and exciting; she did not know how her eyes spar-
kled, or that there was an elfin quality about her face
that the man beside her noticed. . . .

'Have we far to go?' she asked, disconcerted by
his scrutiny and aware of the spread of colour into
her cheeks.

'We have a fair journey, but you will find it
pleasant.' He smiled. 'The *quinta* and the vineyards
are in the valley of the Douro River, where the
mineral content of the soil is just right for the
properties of the grapes.'

'The vintage will start soon,' she reflected, remembering he had said that it always began in
September.

'That's right.' He stopped as his chauffeur said
something to him in Portuguese; he answered, then
lapsed into silence on seeing that Hydee had become
absorbed in the scenery through which they were
passing. The road was tree-lined for as far as the eye
could see; numerous exotic flowers still bloomed in
the hedgerows as they drove along, the tall poplars
rising like sentinels beside them.

At last the Palacio came into view through the
trees. Carlos pointed it out to her as he said casually,
in his low-toned foreign voice, 'There it is, your new
home.'

Her home. . . . She gasped, then stared speech-
lessly, nerves quivering as awe and wonderment
mingled to produce an unwanted tension that almost
deprived her of the ability to appreciate what she
saw. A magnificent building occupying a lush green
plateau on the valley side, it had an essence of
mediaeval grandeur about it, and yet at the same
time there was an impression of mellowed simplicity
which contributed much to its charm. Formal gar-

dens could be seen surrounding it, and these were enhanced by the forest of ancient trees rising majestically as a backcloth both to them and to the Palacio. The gardens spread from the plateau onto a spur; and below this, the vineyards—terraces cut by hand into the valley sides—rose right up to join the farmlands of the *quinta*.

Soon the chauffeur turned the car and they sped down a mile-long avenue of massive umbrella pines after entering through imposing ironwork gates above which was the spreading armorial crest of the Manriques. As they neared the house, she had an immediate impression of vast quiet and beauty, of immaculate care and good taste, of warmth and welcome . . . and of promise.

The car came to a stop on a wide, semicircular forecourt, and moments later Hydee was standing stock-still, looking up at the imposing façade with its large windows, its magnificent doorway, and the pillared verandah running along its whole length. Fountains playing at either side of the forecourt were decorated with carved stonework and *azulejas*—blue and yellow tiles forming pictures which were scenes from Portuguese history. The sweeping lawns, velvet smooth, were divided by long flowerbeds flaring with colour from asters and zinnias, crimson gladioli and deep purple irises. Numerous other flowers added their contribution, and the result was perfection.

She heard her husband give a small cough, was vaguely aware of the chauffeur—whose name was Geraldo—watching her with a sort of amused expression that was yet intensely curious. And she did not know what move to make or what to say. Her mouth was dry, and something cold and aching affected her stomach. For this was not for her—just an ordinary girl who had been jilted, cast off for another. In this mansion would be treasures of the kind she would not dare touch . . . and yet she would be the mistress, wife of a nobleman of impeccable lineage, a proud man, conscious of his inheritance. For a fleeting moment Hydee thought of another girl, Arminda Venancio, who would surely be better fitted for the position than she. How was she going to take the matter of the marriage? Well, there was nothing she could do. It was too late now . . . for everyone. Too late. A terrible fear rose within Hydee's breast, and unconsciously she lifted wide and pleading eyes to meet those of her husband. Sensing her heightened and unpredictable emotions, he immediately dismissed the chauffeur and asked her what was wrong.

'I d-don't belong here,' she stammered, far too upset to feel any embarrassment. She felt she would have given anything to be back in the simple, four-room flat with Ellie, who was keeping it on till her marriage. 'I w-won't fit in. Please . . . .' Her voice faltered helplessly, tears coming closer with every second that passed. She shook her head involuntarily and added in a choked little voice, 'It's d-done now, isn't it, and . . . and it can't b-be undone.'

Much to her surprise, he took her hand, holding it strongly, and she felt then that he was no longer a stranger to her, aloof, distant and unapproachable, but someone close and on whom she could lean if ever the burden of her new life became too heavy for her to bear alone.

'Yes, Hydee, it's done. And once you're used to it here, you'll find you have no regrets. It *is* strange, and it seems so big and perhaps unfriendly—'

'No, not unfriendly,' she was swift to deny. 'Just the reverse, in fact.'

The ghost of a smile touched the fine outline of his mouth, and again she felt she had someone to rely upon.

'Then surely half your misgivings are dissolved? You're right, Hydee, this house does have a warm and friendly atmosphere. It welcomes everyone who cares to visit it, and this you will realise at Christmas when all my relatives—and they're yours, too, now, remember—arrive for the holiday.'

She nodded, managing to hold back the tears that had almost fallen a minute or so ago. 'You're very reassuring, Carlos,' she murmured, aware that this was the first time she had been able to use his name without embarrassment. 'Thank you for helping me to get over my depression.'

'Come,' he said at length. 'You have to meet the servants.'

Another ordeal, but this time she did not feel at all apprehensive. It was as if her husband's action in taking her hand, making physical contact with her, and the kindness of his words, had erased her fears, and she was ready to try her best to assume her new role as the wife of the marquês.

The front door had been opened by the butler, who was introduced to Hydee as Bento; then came Clara, the housekeeper, and Amelia, the cook. There were two housemaids, Ana and Jesuina, and the pretty young girl who had been looking after the children since the last nanny had left. She was Caterina and, said Carlos, she would be Hydee's personal maid. She was nineteen and engaged to Luiz, the head gardener.

'Caterina will show you to our suite.' Carlos's suave words startled her; Hydee turned swiftly, but the question on her lips was stemmed by the warning glance thrown to her by her husband.

'I forgot to tell you we'd be sharing a suite,' he said apologetically a few moments later, having entered the big bedroom she was to occupy. 'It was remiss of me, but no harm's done.'

'I didn't think we'd be so close.' Hydee's anxious eyes strayed past him to the door through which he had entered her room. 'That's a . . . a communicating door?' It was a superfluous question, but she was flustered, Ellie's warning filtering into her mind, the warning that Carlos would assert his rights if he ever felt like it.

'Surely you realised that appearances must be kept up before the servants,' he said rather shortly.

'I didn't give it a thought,' she confessed, a sigh on her lips.

'You'll be quite safe,' he assured her with a trace of amused irony, and it almost seemed to Hydee that he thought she was not good enough for him.

'Yes,' she murmured, 'I know I'll be safe.'

'You don't appear to be too sure,' observed Carlos dryly. 'Do I strike you as a man who would go back on his word?'

She stared up into his proud, aristocratic face, fully conscious of the challenge he had thrown out to her. He was waiting for her answer; she frowned and shook her head bewilderedly because at this moment she was for some inexplicable reason vitally aware of him as a man, of his strength and the impression of latent virility in his lean and sinewed frame.

'I d-don't know,' she answered feebly. 'Ellie said . . .' Too late she stopped; his brows lifted a fraction in a gesture of haughty inquiry.

'What did Ellie say?' His brusque demand was no less disconcerting because it was expected. Hydee looked up into his eyes and asked him to forget it, but he shook his head, repeating the question. She bit her lip, groping for words, and when at last she spoke, it was in a tone of resignation not untinged with anxiety in case she should anger him.

'She said that as we were married it was very likely that . . . that you would . . . would assert your rights.' Warmth and bright crimson rushed into her cheeks. 'I . . . I expect she was wrong though,' added Hydee in an attempt to moderate what she had said.

A brittle silence followed as Carlos stared down into her anxious face, his expression inscrutable except for the humourless, unpleasant smile that twisted his lips.

'Time alone will tell if your friend was wrong,' was all he said. But he added over his shoulder as he moved towards the communicating door, 'We shall dine early tonight—at seven o'clock. In the meantime, do what you like—find your way around.'

She stared at the closed door and wondered bewilderedly why a hurtful cloud of tears had built up behind her eyes.

Chapter Six

The shadows of twilight were veiling the gardens, and the whole aspect was one of peace and tranquillity, with the birds and insects resting after the activities of the day.

Hydee loitered among the flowerbeds, for it was still light enough to appreciate colour and form and beauty. She had been at the Palacio for almost a week and had spent most of the time profitably in exploring her surroundings and in getting to know the servants. She had hoped to see Doreen before she returned to England, but was disappointed. The children would be coming to the Palacio tomorrow, brought by their Aunt Isobella, and for some inexplicable reason Hydee was conscious of a strange feeling of uneasiness which at times actually overshadowed the excitement with which she awaited the arrival of the children. It was nothing tangible that caused her to be apprehensive of the meeting with her husband's sister, and yet, subconsciously, she expected it to be an ordeal.

However, she told herself that nothing could be gained by idle speculation, and she managed to thrust her new and unknown sister-in-law from her mind and to concentrate instead on the glories of nature which surrounded her. The grounds were so vast and rambling that there were still regions she had not explored, and now she directed her steps away from what had become familiar and proceeded towards an arched wrought-iron gateway above which was the Manrique crest in red and gold. It led to a pathway made shady and silent by the interlacing branches of the stately laurel trees overhead. She walked on, savouring the peace, her mind now and then insistently bringing the face and figure of her husband before her eyes.

For the past three days she had known strange stirrings of pulse and heart when in his presence. She was becoming aware of his maleness and magnetism . . . and of the fact that he was her husband. . . .

Determinedly concentrating on where she was going, she continued along the path for another few minutes before stopping abruptly with a gasp of pleasure and appreciation. Before her was an exquisite little fountain whose waters were dancing in an oval, wide-edged pool along which were earthenware pots containing sweetly perfumed flowers and small trees with yellow and crimson foliage. Around the outside edge were charming stone benches, their high backs decorated with the branching coat-of-arms of the Manrique family. Fish darted about in the crystal-clear water, and even in the fading light their colours could be seen and Hydee surmised they would be iridescent when caught in sunlight. Another path caught her eye, and she moved to look along it. Its entire length was a stupendous mass of colour from the thousands of dahlias bordering its sides, and at the end was a gazebo constructed in the form of a Doric temple. Between its fluted columns were windows around which jasmine grew in abundance. What a picture it would make when the flowers were in full bloom in the late spring and early summer!

'Oh, but I'm looking forward to the thrill of seeing each season come and go!' she said aloud. 'What a lot I have to look forward to—' Her voice died abruptly as a sound caught her ears. She swung round, heart thumping. 'Oh . . . it's you. . . .' Her sigh of relief was almost audible.

'You're going to be caught in the dark.' Carlos's voice was smoothly impersonal as he came up to her from behind. 'Have you not been along here before?'

She shook her head, pulses fluttering. He was close—too close; she could smell his after-shave mingling pervasively with his own male fragrance, and the startling knowledge invaded her mind that she was fighting an emotion that was physical desire.

Desire. . . . Shyness and embarrassment swept through her, and she could not lift her eyes to meet his gaze lest she reveal what her emotions were. How furious he would be if he were to read her mind, to discover that in this short period of time she had found him attractive.

'I asked you a question, Hydee,' he reminded her, and before she quite knew what was happening, she felt the hard pressure of his long lean fingers as he tilted her head back, forcing her to meet his all-examining eyes. The contact with his flesh sent a quiver of pleasure rippling along her spine. She wanted those fingers to move from beneath her chin to her throat, to hypersensitive places she had learned about when she was engaged to Noel. She wanted to feel his hand cupping her breast, his moist lips exploring it. . . . Hot colour flooded her cheeks, and she sprang away from him, ashamed and angry at her secret thoughts and wishing with all her heart she had not decided on this particular exploration but had kept to the more public part of the grounds.

'I haven't been in this part before.' She managed at last to answer his question, vitally aware of his frowning puzzlement at her action in springing away from him so abruptly. But why had he touched her? His manner with her was always one of cool politeness, yet just now he had actually made what could only be described as an intimate gesture, proprietary, as if she really were his wife in every sense.

He made no response to her quiet words, and an uneasy silence dropped between them as they stood there looking at the gazebo, its mellowed stone dark and shadowed as twilight dissolved into the enveloping folds of night. Suddenly all Hydee's tensions were dissolved, too, as if the mothy darkness had provided a protective barrier against her unwanted emotions and impossible desires.

'Shall we make our way back?' Carlos broke the silence at last, and she lifted her eyes to meet his. 'You'll not want to stay out here alone, surely?' No concern in his voice, and no interest, either. Hydee wondered if his attitude towards her would change once his children were back with him.

'No, of course not.' She fell into step beside him as he moved, taking the way past the fountain and pool to enter the path bordered by the high laurels. There was just sufficient room for them to walk side by side, and although she did not suppose he would be happy if their bodies touched, she also knew that he would not expect her to walk a few paces behind him. Of course, she could have gone on in front, but she chose to keep by his side, becoming intensely aware, as they went along, that the barrier protecting her emotions was being effectively attacked; she was vitally alive to his nearness and the intimacy that it inevitably created in her receptive senses. She deliberately moved so that her body rubbed against his; she let her hand touch his, and hoped he would presume it to be by accident rather than the deliberate act that it was.

Throbbing pulse and racing heartbeats; yearning and desire in a riot of conflicting emotions that threatened to sweep away all control and lead her to remind her husband that they were in reality on their honeymoon! What was the matter with her that this feeling had come with such force and turbulence? Why hadn't it come slowly, almost imperceptibly at first, so that she would have been warned and armed and able to quench the fire even before it began to smoulder? As it was, she felt herself to be consumed by flames that could in the end destroy her altogether, because there was no hope of reciprocation on her husband's part, no future for them physically. . . .

Or was there? Perhaps, but if ever Carlos did take her, asserting his rights as prophesied by her friend, it would be done on impulse to assuage a craving of the flesh, and she would be left hurt and bruised and nursing an aching heart. It would be far better to make sure that she never gave away her secret, never allowed him to suspect that he would meet with success should he make approaches, reminding her that she was his wife.

They walked on in silence; the sun's last lingering light had gone, but the moon was up, creating a scene of celestial splendour, with intrepid stars piercing the indigo as the sky darkened swiftly over the gardens and vineyards and the river below.

'I'll see you at dinner,' Carlos said as they entered the Palacio at last.

'Yes,' she returned briefly, and left him, ascending the magnificent balustraded stiarcase while he strode away to the end of the great hall where his study was located in the west wing of the house.

The children arrived the following afternoon, and Hydee was introduced to their aunt. Isobella's manner was cold, but her brother seemed not to notice, and within a couple of minutes of her arrival he was called to the telephone, leaving the two women with the children, who immediately decided to go out to the garden and play. Isobella moved with the grace and sleekness of a cat and took possession of a chair. Hydee looked at her from a small distance, noticing the impassive face and black, long-lashed eyes below curving brows. Her skin was dark and clear, her neck arched above gently sloping shoulders. Pride was written in every line and curve of the slender body, and Hydee disliked her with an intensity that seemed absurd, since they were still strangers.

'Your marriage to my brother came as a shock,' the woman said at last, her tone glacier cold, her eyes narrowed and glinting. 'We all suspected that

Carlos would take a step like that, but we hoped the new marquesa would fit the position she was to occupy. But you . . .'

Blood rushed to Hydee's cheeks at the outspoken-ness of the woman who was her sister-in-law, the contemptuous words stinging more painfully than the lash of a whip. But by some miracle Hydee remained both calm and dignified, for she was suddenly determined not to let herself be regarded as inferior, even though she felt she was unfit for the position she now occupied.

'As I am sure you regret your uncalled-for rude-ness just now, I will allow it to pass. As for your remark about my marriage to your brother coming as a shock—well, as you had no idea whom he was marrying, and as you had never set eyes on me until a few moments ago, I'm afraid I'm baffled as to exactly what you mean.'

It was Isobella's turn to colour up, and in that moment Hydee knew she had made an enemy, for dark venom looked out from her eyes, and her mouth was twisted into an ugly, almost evil line. 'You're impertinent!' she hissed. 'You're a nobody—a girl who's obviously congratulating herself on having landed a millionaire, with a title thrown in as a bonus!'

Hydee could only stare, trying to maintain her dignity and to hit back in a way this woman would understand. It seemed incredible that she could be so uncontrolled and cruel, and Hydee felt sure there must be some very good reason for it.

'I think,' she said coldly at length, 'that we had better not carry on this . . . er . . . conversation any longer. I must go and join my stepchildren, who, I am sure, have been waiting eagerly to come home to join their father and me. It's hardly fair to leave them out there. If you will excuse me . . .'

'Just a minute!' Isobella's voice was harsh and commanding; it was also strongly accented, which it had not been before. 'When I said my brother's marriage to you was a shock, I meant that we had heard he had married someone who had applied for the post of nanny—'

'Who told you that?' broke in Hydee, then realised it must have been Doreen, who, no doubt, had merely mentioned it in passing, never for one moment suspecting it would be used in this derogatory way.

'It isn't important,' snapped Isobella tautly. 'My brother ought to have chosen a woman who was his equal; we all expected it of him, and as he knew this, we naturally took it for granted that he would respect our wishes!'

Hydee could not help smiling. 'I should have thought you would know your brother better than that,' she said. 'Carlos is not the man to be told what to do.' Had he chosen her, Hydee, as an act of defiance towards his relatives? she wondered, then immediately rejected the idea. Carlos would not be so petty. He had chosen her for no other reason than that he considered she would be a suitable person to bring up his children—with his help, of course.

'There is another woman who would have suited him far better.' Isobella's voice was scarcely audible, and Hydee realised she was talking to herself.

She said quietly, 'It was plain that Carlos did not consider this other woman to be suitable.'

'As a nanny?' with a raising of the immaculately trimmed eyebrows. 'That is all you are; I suppose you realise that?'

'The children will soon come to regard me as their stepmother,' replied Hydee with conviction and dignity.

'An optimist, eh?' Isobella's sudden laugh was in effect a sneer. 'How long do you expect to last? There have been other nannies—'

'Perhaps,' interrupted Hydee, looking straight at her, 'you will tell me what this is all about?'

There was a glacial silence before the Portuguese woman spoke. She had been debating, Hydee thought, and her words served to strengthen this idea.

'I was a very great friend of Eunice, his first wife. I am also a friend of the woman who expected to marry him: Arminda Venancio. You are an interloper in my eyes, and I am sure that all Carlos's relations will regard you in the same light. You'll never fit in,' she added contemptuously, casting her eyes over Hydee's slender figure before deliberately bringing them back to rest upon her face. 'A lowborn—what was he thinking about!' The words were spat out from lips that were twisted with fury. 'I wouldn't give the marriage more than six months at the most!'

Hydee, very pale now and trembling, looked at Isobella for a long moment in silence before, turning on her heel, she left the room and went out to join the children.

It was ten days later that Hydee met Arminda Venancio. The other woman drove up to the front of the Palacio in a long black car which she brought to a stop on the forecourt. Hydee was in her bedroom, standing at the window. She was free until half-past three, when the children came home from the small private school which they attended five days a week. Hydee's eyes flickered with perception as she looked down, instinctively knowing that this was the woman who had hoped to marry Carlos. She was small and dainty, her steps swift and urgent as she hurried from the car to the door of the Palacio. Hydee stared broodingly at the car, her thoughts turning to her encounter with her husband's sister. Those blatant insults seemed unbelievable, looked at in retrospect. Isobella might have breeding, and blue blood in her veins, but her manners certainly left a great deal to be desired. What would Carlos say if he knew how his wife had been treated? He had seemed to get along very well with Isobella, and Hydee had no doubts about her being able to effectively hide her shortcomings from him.

A quiet knock on her bedroom door brought her head around. 'Come in,' she invited, and Caterina entered.

'The senhor wishes to see you,' she said with her usual ready smile. Small and dark, with flashing eyes widely set below delicately curving brows, Caterina was a most attractive girl in Hydee's opinion. Her disposition was carefree and lively; she was eager to please in every way, while at the same time respecting Hydee's wishes for privacy. She had learned never to appear when Hydee was dressing or in the bath. She was observant, and Hydee felt sure that she had guessed that Carlos never visited his wife. But Hydee was also sure that whatever Caterina suspected was never talked about to any of the other servants.

'Thank you, Caterina,' she returned graciously. 'I'll be down directly.' She paused a moment in a mood of indecision. 'Er . . . he has a visitor with him, I think?'

Caterina's face was impassive as she said, 'Yes, Dona Hydee, he has.'

Hydee licked her lips. She ought not to put questions to her maid. Carlos would be furious at such undignified behavior, but of course, he would never know. Hydee just had to ask about Arminda, because she very much feared she would be equally as hostile towards her as Isobella had been.

'The young lady is a very good friend of Dom Carlos, I believe?'

Caterina nodded, looking straight at her. Silence reigned for a space before she said in a quiet, respectful voice, 'We all thought that the senhorita would marry Dom Carlos. They were very good friends, as you say, senhora, but it was obvious that Dom Carlos did not love her, and so he married you.'

'She comes from an illustrious family, I'm told.'

'But, senhora,' said Caterina in the same respectful voice, 'it is not always breeding that is important. Dom Carlos's servants are very happy that he married you and not Dona Arminda.'

Hydee looked at her through eyes that were suddenly bright. 'Thank you, Caterina,' she murmured simply, and went past her from the room, leaving her to close the door behind her.

'Ah, there you are.' Carlos smiled as Hydee entered, and beckoned her over to where the Portuguese woman was standing, her aristocratic features rather drawn, her dark eyes brooding and dull. Hydee cast her husband a searching glance, wondering what had passed between him and Arminda before he sent for her to join them. He met her eyes, but she read nothing from the mask that had fallen over them.

Carlos introduced them; Hydee saw the woman flinch when Carlos mentioned the word 'wife.' Her handshake was surprisingly limp and conventional, her manners rather better than those of her friend, for she murmured a polite 'How do you do? Your marriage to Carlos came as a surprise to many people.'

She was bearing up well, thought Hydee, admiring her for it while at the same time aware that she could never like the girl. Her disdain was too obvious; like Isobella, she considered Hydee to be the most unsuitable woman Carlos could ever have chosen as a wife.

'Arminda's been away in Lisbon,' explained Carlos, 'and so she only heard of our marriage last night when she arrived back and Isobella phoned her.'

Arminda lifted her eyes and said, as if she had forgotten Hydee's presence altogether, 'It was an awful shock, Carlos.'

He seemed to swallow something in his throat. Hydee suddenly wanted to escape, to leave them together . . . and yet at the same time a spasm of jealousy shot through her.

The moment was tense, electric. Arminda was the one to ease it by saying it was time she left, as her mother was waiting to be driven into town.

'We have only one car now, as you know,' she added finally, with a thin smile for Carlos.

'We shall see you and Dona Lucia soon—at our dinner party?'

'Of course. Mother and I will be pleased to come.' Her face was pale, her lips compressed. Hydee felt sorry for her but knew why Carlos had not chosen her for his wife.

There was a hardness about her that he could not possibly miss; he knew she would never make a suitable mother for his children. But for all that, Hydee was of the firm conviction that what he felt for Arminda was something far deeper than mere friendship.

Chapter Seven

It was from Gasper that Hydee learned more about Arminda. He called the following day, and as the vintage was in full swing, Carlos was away from the house, supervising the activities which began at daybreak with an army of workers invading the *quinta* from the surrounding countryside, eager to earn some extra money. Men, women and even children came, dancing along to the rhythm of guitars and mandolins, a merry crowd which seemed to turn the vintage into a carnival.

Standing on a shady verandah, Hydee saw the white, low-slung sports car arrive, and the way in which the driver slewed it to an abrupt standstill gave the immediate impression of a devil-may-care attitude towards life. Yet the figure of the man himself was impressive, his every movement stamping him a member of the nobility. With a frowning gaze Hydee watched him approach the house, covering the distance with the same athletic grace that was so familiar because Carlos, too, moved in that lithely powerful way. Another member of the family? Involuntarily Hydee's mouth tightened; she had no wish to meet this man, and she was about to retreat into the room behind her when, chancing to look up, he caught sight of her, smiled and waved, and called something which she failed to catch. Biting her lip in vexation, she pondered the possibility of making some excuse when the servant informed her of the man's appearance. But after only a moment's thought she shrugged resignedly, admitting that there was no alternative than to meet him, and she proceeded to the drawing room to wait his entry into the house. He was shown in by Bento, who began in his customary accented but stolid voice, 'The Visconde Gasper Antonio Joao—'

'That'll do,' broke in the young man with a wry expression sent in Hydee's direction. 'You can go, but bring me in a glass of sherry in about five minutes.'

The man went, closing the door silently behind him, and the two stood staring at one another before Gasper said in the same impeccable English, 'Hello, my new cousin-in-law!' He strode towards her, his hand outstretched, his slate-grey eyes meeting hers, which were wide and limpid and scanning his aristocratic face anxiously for some sign of disfavour even while instinct told her she would find none, that here was a member of the illustrious family who was far different from Isobella. He was smiling as she gave him her small white hand, and he said sincerely, 'Welcome to our country and our family. I would have come sooner but, like Arminda, I have been away.' Tall and assured, he stood smiling down at her, and suddenly her heart was light.

'I'm happy to meet you, Gasper. Carlos told me about you—and about the other members of his family.' She paused, then added, 'Carlos is not here, but I can send for him if you want me to.'

'It's not Carlos I have come to see, but you.' He glanced at a low couch below the window. 'Shall we sit down?'

'Of course.' Why had he come to see her? she wondered, taking a seat on the couch and watching him bring up a chair so that he would be sitting opposite her instead of beside her.

'The other members . . .' Gasper gave her his full attention, a wry expression in his dark grey eyes. 'And what did you think of my cousin Isobella?' he inquired, watching her curiously, interested in her reaction to his mention of his cousin.

'You've been speaking to her?' she countered at once, and he nodded without hesitation. 'She doesn't like me,' Hydee then added, a quiver in her voice. 'But if she's been talking to you about me, then you know what her feelings are.' She looked at him through troubled eyes. 'I can understand her sentiments,' she went on when he did not speak. 'She had other ideas for her brother.'

'Big ideas,' submitted Gasper. 'But she should know Carlos better than to think she can influence him.' Gasper turned as the door opened and Bento entered carrying a small silver tray on which was the glass of sherry.

'Aren't you having anything?' he asked, and Hydee shook her head.

'No, thank you.' She watched the servant leave, then turned her attention to Gasper again, examining his features and approving of them, for although he had the same athletic build as his cousin, the same stamp of the nobility, here the resemblance ended. Gasper's features were softer, his eyes serious at this moment, but she knew they would laugh often; his mouth was firm yet wide and generous, and she sensed that it could purse with compassion just as easily as it could curve with humour. The moment he had come across the room, extending a hand, she had been strangely affected by him, and by the sure knowledge that she had at last found a friend. 'Why have you come?' she inquired as he put the glass to his lips.

'Because, Hydee, I realised that you might require some support. You're a brave girl to have married my cousin. Surely you had some misgivings?'

She nodded, replying mechanically, 'At first, yes, I suppose I did.' Unconsciously she played with a few strands of hair; it was a nervous gesture acquired since her marriage. 'You say I might need support. . . .' She broke off, reluctant to proceed, and seeing her embarrassment, Gasper began to talk, dispensing with tact.

'Isobella learned of the circumstances of your marriage, and so you must be prepared for the whole family to know that it was a marriage of convenience. They now realize that Carlos, having become convinced that it was a mother his children needed rather than a nanny, embarked on this unorthodox method of procuring one.' He paused a moment to put his glass down on the table. 'Don't be embarrassed with me,' he said gently. 'I'm the odd one out in this family, not approved of, as you will very soon discover. And so it seemed to me—after listening to the bitter complaints of Isobella regarding her brother's marriage—that I had better see you and forewarn you as to what to expect.'

'It was thoughtful of you,' she murmured, but went on to add that he must realise that what he was saying was a great embarrassment to her.

'It shouldn't be,' he returned. 'If you accept that I know all about this marriage, then we can discuss things together openly and easily. I'm only here because I firmly believe you ought to know that there's at least one member of the family who doesn't disapprove of you.'

'You're very kind, Gasper.' She looked at him mistily, quite unaware of the dark, troubled expression in her eyes, of the faint convulsive movement of her mouth. 'But please don't get everything wrong,' she begged. 'Carlos is very nice to me, very kind.'

'He would have to be, wouldn't he? After all, he prevailed on you to marry him, to enter this business deal which is to affect your whole future. Yes, surely he must be kind to you.' Sharp the last few words, and an unexpected hardness entered his eyes, reminding her of Carlos.

'I wanted to marry him,' she readily confessed. And before she quite knew it, she was confiding in him, telling him that she had been alone in the world after having been jilted. And lastly she heard herself say, 'I would never have looked at another man after Noel—not in the ordinary way—but yet I wanted to be with children, so I snatched this chance to become a mother.'

'And you've no regrets?' he asked curiously.

'None.' Not yet . . . but would she have eventually? 'Carlos doesn't seem to be aware of Isobella's true character, does he?' Hydee changed the subject, breaking the silence that had fallen between them.

'Some women have the ability to adopt a front to suit the situation. You'll have different treatment from her when Carlos is around,' he predicted.

'She was a great friend of Carlos's first wife—so she said.'

'She actually told you that?' Gasper frowned in disgust. 'Yes, she and Eunice were exceptionally friendly, and yet Isobella showed little emotion when she died.'

'She's now friendly with Arminda.' Although rather reluctant to discuss these people, Hydee was at the same time exceedingly curious to learn more about them. 'She had hoped Carlos would marry her.'

Gasper nodded, putting his glass to his lips and regarding Hydee thoughtfully from above its rim. 'You've met Arminda, I believe?' And when she inclined her head, he added, 'Isobella lost no time in contacting her on her return from Lisbon. Arminda has been backed as the second marquesa ever since she and her mother took up residence in this district, and I must admit that I myself expected something to come from the friendship that instantly sprang up between Arminda and my cousin. However, Carlos, in one of his infrequent expansive moods, actually confided to me that he could never marry Arminda, simply because he was sure she would not devote herself to the children. She's been used to a full social life, and marriage to Carlos would have provided the opportunity for her to resume that life, at least as she saw things. Also, she has her mother hanging on all the time, another reason why Carlos discarded the idea of marrying her.'

Hydee, having listened with interest, glanced away to look through the massive side window to where tall umbrella pines shaded part of the garden where Luiz was working. All was kept immaculate out there, with the verdant carpet of the lawn patterned with beds of exotic flowers blooming in the warm afternoon sunshine. But although her attention was with the beauty she saw, Hydee was trying to speak, to voice something that was proving very difficult, but at last she heard herself say, as she turned from the window, 'I had the impression that Carlos cares a great deal for Arminda.'

Gasper nodded in agreement, and Hydee felt a stab of jealousy, realising it was the second time she had been affected in this way.

'I'm sure he cares a lot about her, and he'd have married her if it hadn't been for the reasons I've mentioned. Carlos has many faults, but his love for his children, and his sense of duty towards them, carry far more weight with him than any personal feelings or desires.'

So he was probably in love with Arminda, just as Hydee had suspected. . . . 'What was Carlos's first wife like?' she asked presently. 'She was English, too.'

'I detested her,' he admitted quite frankly. 'Carlos was only twenty when he married her. He's a passionate man—or at least he was then—and she found favour with him in that particular way. They were married for several years before Ramos was born, and I expect they were happy.' He spread his hands. 'I don't know. But after the birth of Luisa, they seemed to drift apart, and she definitely had lovers. Isobella doesn't know this, but I do.'

Hydee frowned at the information. '*How* do you know?' she asked, the frown still between her eyes.

'Because, unfortunately for women, men talk.'

'Did Carlos know?'

'I expect he did; one would have the greatest difficulty in keeping anything from Carlos.'

'Yet he continued to live with her?'

'Here in Portugal we don't favour divorce, as you probably know.'

Hydee was silent, her thoughts shifting to Isobella's prophecy that Hydee's marriage would not last six months.

'But in the end, there was no love between Carlos and his wife?' she murmured at last, speaking to herself rather than to her companion.

'I don't believe there was real, deep love even in the beginning. Eunice married for wealth and position and he for . . . well, the convenience of having a woman at hand.' Gasper broke off, grinning at her expression before he went on, 'In our family—and many like it—love is not considered essential to a successful marriage. We're a hard, mercenary lot, and you'll find that Carlos is no different from the rest of us.'

She looked at him almost with affection and stated firmly, '*You* are different, Gasper, and I'm sure that when you marry it will be for love.'

'Think so?' His eyes rested on her face for a long,

unfathomable moment. 'Well, that's in the far future, because I assure you that my bachelor life appeals to me at present. I like the freedom. I've just been to Paris and had a rather wonderful time with a glamourous blonde I met there while on another visit five months ago.' He laughed at Hydee's rising colour. 'If I were married I'd not be able to gallivant about like that.' Picking up his glass, he took a drink, then stared absently into the amber liquid that was left, appearing to be deep in thought.

After long moments Hydee said, thinking of Isobella and speaking her thoughts aloud, 'It's not going to be very pleasant unless Isobella changes her opinion of me, is it?'

'She'll not change,' he said firmly. And then, after a small hesitation, 'It was a shock, as you can imagine, when—after the whole family had decided that Arminda was the girl for Carlos—he brought home an English bride he had married without ceremony.' Gasper broke off and laughed.

To her surprise, Hydee found herself laughing too as she said, feigning indignation, 'I assure you we *did* have a ceremony!'

'In a way I can understand Isobella's feelings,' conceded Gasper when their laughter had died, 'but I certainly don't sympathise with them.'

The assurance was unnecessary; his earlier remarks had already convinced Hydee that he had no time at all for Isobella.

'I'm glad you came today,' she murmured, casting him a look of gratitude, and for no reason at all she thought of Noel and recalled the happiness they had once enjoyed. Their happiness had seemed so strong and permanent that nothing, just nothing, could take

it away. Yet both were now married to other people. . . . Unwanted tears filled her eyes, and Gasper,
misunderstanding the reason for them, impulsively
leant forward and placed a hand over hers as it
rested on the arm of the sofa.

'Don't take Isobella's vicious words to heart,' he
advised gently. 'As I've said, it took courage to
marry Carlos; and you just hang on to that courage
so that you can stand up to Isobella, and the rest of
the family, too. I don't suppose you've met Ines
yet?'

Hydee shook her head, aware from his tone that
Ines was another Isobella. She was the daughter of
Gasper's Aunt Gracinha and Uncle Duarte, who
owned a *palacio* and *quinta* about half the size of
Carlos's.

'She's recently been married.'

'That's right—married a visconde named Francisco, whom you'll detest on sight. No love match,
that,' he assured her with a wry grimace. 'Money—
on both sides, an amalgamation of wealth with no
thought to emotions or the eventual drifting apart
which so often results from marriages of that kind.'

'They'll all be our guests at Christmas, so Carlos
said. I hope, Gasper, that you will be here.'

'You can rely on me,' was Gasper's staunch reply,
which made Hydee feel totally uplifted, and also that
she had known him for weeks at least. He was
charming; he could be frivolous, she surmised, and
yet he had an equally attractive serious side which
was the basis of her confidence that, if it should ever
be necessary, he would be her friend and her prop.
As for her own attitude towards him, she was faintly
surprised at her ability to be totally uninhibited, but

his manner was so easy and spontaneous that it would in any case have been impossible for her to have felt uncomfortable for very long.

His hand still lay on top of hers; his eyes were wide and strangely fixed. She fluttered him a smile and discovered that, somehow, he had come closer so that she felt his cool breath on her cheek.

And it was at that very moment that the door swung inwards and they saw Carlos standing in the entranceway, having stopped abruptly on capturing the scene—the two sitting there, close, and looking into each other's eyes.

'Good afternoon, Gasper,' he said with cold politeness. 'Is there some particular reason why you are holding my wife's hand?'

Gasping at his lack of delicacy, Hydee snatched her hand away, colour leaping to her cheeks.

'None except that we're getting acquainted,' replied Gasper smoothly.

Coming farther into the room, Carlos stood by the fireplace, one arm resting in what seemed a casual manner on the mantelshelf. 'What time did you arrive?' Carlos's eyes went briefly to the sherry glass which was standing empty on a small table at his cousin's elbow.

'I've been here for about an hour.'

'Why didn't you send for me?' There was a trace of censure mingling with the arrogance in his tone which Gasper chose to ignore.

'I didn't come to see you, Carlos; I'd been speaking to Isobella and decided to come along and introduce myself to your charming wife.' Was there a challenge in the words? Hydee felt uncomfortable and lowered her eyes.

'I'm giving a dinner party so that you can all meet

Hydee,' returned Carlos in cold tones. And, after a slight pause during which his gaze was fixed, unmoving, on his wife's bent head, 'You decided to come after talking with Isobella, you said?'

'That's right.' Hydee glanced up swiftly, her nerves drawn tight as she feared Gasper would say too much to his cousin. But she need not have worried; he caught her pleading glance and added mildly, 'As long as Isobella had informed me of your marriage, it would have seemed wrong if I'd not come over at once to meet my new cousin.' He looked all charm at this moment, a half-smile on his lips, a glimmer of good humour in his slate-grey eyes. 'I think you must agree with me, Carlos?'

Watching her husband's expression, Hydee was filled with misgivings without being able to explain them. He seemed so stern, so vexed that his cousin had called. She supposed it was not the thing for Gasper to be holding her hand like that, and yet why should Carlos care? She was nothing to him, and it wasn't as if Gasper had shown his affection in front of company.

'As I said,' returned Carlos, the piercing curtness of his voice cutting the atmosphere, 'I intend to give a dinner party so that Hydee can be formally introduced to the family.'

'She doesn't particularly want to be introduced formally,' Gasper took it on himself to state. 'This kind of introduction's far less unnerving than being confronted by a host of strangers all at once.'

'I think it is I who shall decide what is good for my wife.' Etched into Carlos' austere features was a harsh, uncompromising quality which sent an involuntary shiver along Hydee's spine. However, as Gasper chose not to comment, the awkward moment passed, and for the next few minutes the two men talked inconsequentially about the vintage, and then Gasper rose from his chair.

'I shall see you both at the dinner party.' He smiled reassuringly at Hydee and went out.

Carlos looked at his wife across the distance separating them and said coldly, 'Gasper's the family's flirt—but I assume you gathered that much?' There could be no doubt as to his meaning. Hydee averted her head, aware of a little access of anger rising within her because of his attitude. At this moment he was like his sister: arrogant, distant, superior.

'I found him pleasant to talk to,' she responded quietly. 'He certainly didn't do anything I could resent.' Despite her frayed temper, she was nervous; it was an uncomfortable feeling, which she tried vainly to shake off.

'Gasper doesn't like my sister.' Carlos spoke brusquely, making no comment on what she had said. 'What did he have to say about her?'

'Nothing much,' she prevaricated, and saw at once that it was not the answer her husband had asked for. His frowning gaze bit into her, and his mouth, compressed into a thin line, seemed almost cruel. 'Isobella doesn't like me,' she continued, then stopped as he made a swift gesture as if to repudiate the statement.

'It's Gasper who doesn't like her,' he corrected. His eyes were coldly curious as he repeated, 'What did he have to say about her?'

'It was nothing derogatory,' she murmured, a dryness catching at her throat.

'Derogatory,' he repeated, and there was no mistaking the significance of the word. Hydee knew she had made a slip, one which she realised could not be rectified.

But what must she do? To repeat what Gasper had said was unthinkable. 'I'd rather not carry on this conversation,' she offered at last, conscious of a little twinge of desolation at the coldness of her husband towards her. For the past few days she had desired to be closer to him, to cement their friendship, but at the same time she had been deterred from making any approach because she had begun to wonder if he felt any real respect for her. Perhaps, deep within him, he despised her, feeling, as his sister did, that she was of low birth when compared to his own noble lineage, which, Hydee knew, could be traced back for a thousand years. 'Please don't ask me these questions, Carlos,' she added pleadingly.

'I shall question Gasper, then.'

She lapsed into silence, and within a few minutes she was alone, her eyes misty, a weight on her heart which seemed almost to be physical.

She wrote to Ellie the following day, her letter bright and full of news of the children, and in the end she mentioned the dinner party which Carlos was shortly to give. Hydee wrote lightly of the coming event, but she was quailing inwardly, convinced that it would be an ordeal which she would not forget in a hurry.

And she was right. The massive dining salon of the Palacio was brilliant with lights, mostly concealed except for the candles on the long glittering table, set in silver-gilt candelabra. Flowers in the centre were matched in miniature at the ladies' places. Crystal, fine antique porcelain, hand-embroidered napkins and table mats . . . Hydee had stood watching Ana and Jesuina putting the finishing touches to the table and knew without any doubt at all that she would be glad when the evening came to an end.

Chapter Eight

It happened that the first two guests to arrive were Arminda and her mother, the older woman tall and erect, superbly dressed in a long black velvet gown trimmed with diamanté studs; she was regal, with all the arrogant confidence of a queen. She met Hydee's gaze as they shook hands, and in the black depths Hydee read, unmistakably, a dark venomous hatred that sent an uncomfortable quiver running along her spine. Hydee flushed under the prolonged unsmiling stare and swallowed convulsively, wishing she were a thousand miles away. Arminda merely inclined her head and moved with the same regal grace as her mother, accepting the chair which Carlos offered to her. Immaculate in evening dress, he fitted in so perfectly that Hydee did not merely feel herself to be the odd one out but admitted quite freely that she was.

'Whereabouts in England do you come from?' Dona Lucia inquired in tones of icy politeness.

Hydee told her, wondering if her voice sounded as strange to her listener as it did to her own ears. Arminda was talking to Carlos, who, having brought her a drink, bent to hand it to her, and their heads seemed to Hydee to be far too close. They were speaking quietly, with only a murmur crossing the room to reach Hydee. Arminda's eyes were faintly accusing but wide and appealing, too.

It was another ten minutes before the next guests arrived, and Hydee had in some measure calmed down by then, having made a tremendous effort to pull herself together. Her subconscious had warned her that unless she was to appear as totally characterless, she must keep up some kind of a front. She felt that Carlos ought to help her, but on the arrival of four additional friends he merely introduced her and went back to Arminda; he perched himself on the arm of her chair until the arrival of Isobella, who had come without her husband, the excuse being that he was unwell and had decided at the last minute to go to bed.

Isobella seated herself next to Hydee on the cushioned sofa and waited for her drink to be served by Bento. Carlos, from his place in the middle of the room, watched his sister closely. Isobella began to chat to Hydee and to smile, and had she not been warned by Gasper, Hydee would have been at a loss to account for the change in the woman's attitude towards her. As Gasper had predicted, Isobella did not intend to let her brother see just how much she disliked her new sister-in-law. Later, however, she said softly, an invidious note in her voice, 'Well, do you now accept that you're totally out-of-place here?'

'I'm Carlos's wife,' returned Hydee stiffly through whitened lips. Isobella's answer to this was merely a sneer.

Ines and her husband, Francisco, arrived and were formally presented to Hydee, who realised at once that Isobella had been talking to them, because their eyes swept her with contempt. A nanny, they were thinking—a servant and yet a relative.

Other guests arrived, including one of Carlos's aunts, an overweight woman with silver hair piled high on her head and a face as arrogant as the rest. Her handclasp was damp and limp.

'So you're the English girl we've all been brought here to see.' Her pale protuberant eyes slid with cold hauteur from the top of Hydee's head to her feet, and a deep sigh escaped the woman before, turning away, she spoke to one of the other guests, saying, 'Ah, Antonia, how are you? And how are your charming children?'

So much for the snub. How many more would come her way before the evening was out? wondered Hydee.

But at last, just when she was telling herself that he would not come, Gasper arrived, his tall striking figure clad in an off-white suit with a frilled shirt and a black bow tie. He stood for a moment by the door, his eyes scanning the room until they settled on Hydee's flushed face. With no more than a nod to his cousin, he strode through the brilliant throng of guests until he reached her side.

'Hydee,' he greeted her, his ready smile succeeding in its intent to lift her spirits and bring a swift, winning response to lips that had been quivering only seconds ago. His hands came out to clasp hers; he bent to brush her cheek with his lips. 'How charming you look!' he exclaimed. 'Blue is definitely your colour.' His eyes met hers in a steady and reassuring gaze. Her own eyes, limpid and appealing, thanked him, but she spoke, too, saying with a dignity and assurance she had lacked from the moment of the appearance of the first two guests, 'Thank you, Gasper. I'm so glad to see you arrive.'

'I'm flattered, my dear.' For a fleeting second he let his eyes dart to Isobella's face, and then, deliberately turning his back on her, and keeping hold of Hydee's hand, he led her over to a vacant couch and they sat down.

Bento came at once, speaking in Portuguese. Gasper answered in English, haughtily, as if admonishing Bento for not being more polite to his mistress.

'Dry sherry, Bento.' Gasper looked at Hydee. 'For you?'

'I left my drink over there.'

'Bento will get you another.'

His smile was inordinately attractive, filling his eyes with warmth.

'Has she said anything to you?' he wanted to know when Bento had gone, and he inclined his head in Isobella's direction so that there could be no question as to whom he meant.

'She's . . . insulting, Gasper. . . .' Hydee's voice trailed off because she knew she ought not to be saying such things to Gasper; it was disloyal to Carlos, who seemed to be quite fond of his sister.

'In what way?' asked Gasper softly. 'Tell me about it.'

She shook her head. 'It doesn't matter—' she began, but he interrupted her.

'Certainly it matters. Carlos didn't bring you here to be insulted by his relatives. She's poison, always has been if she can't get all her own way. She set her heart on a match between her friend Arminda and Carlos, and it hasn't come off. She's seething but helpless.' Gasper leant closer because Arminda's mother had sauntered over and was standing rather close, for no apparent reason. 'Isobella never lets anything rest, and she'll continue to insult you. Don't let her acid tongue upset you,' he advised, his mouth close to her ear. 'And always remember, Hydee, that you have at least one friend in this family—me. Tomorrow, when Carlos is away, I shall call for you and show you my home. Come and visit me just whenever you like.'

She nodded, happy at his words about being her friend. 'I feel so much better now that you're here,' she confessed, giving him a lovely smile and then letting it fade when she noticed her husband's expression as her eyes caught his. He was staring at her with a scowl on his hard, inflexible face, his darkly brilliant eyes appearing almost black as they stared piercingly into hers before moving with a kind of insidious slowness to the face of his cousin. Hydee lowered her lashes, and the next moment Gasper was speaking and she promptly forgot the rather frightening look her husband had given her.

At the table she had Gasper sitting opposite her, and they chatted like old friends while many arrogant and disapproving eyes looked on.

Although Carlos spoke to her often, bringing her

into the conversation with a smile on his lips, she was profoundly conscious of the fact that his main interest lay with Arminda, who was sitting a little farther along the table from Gasper, and it was to her pale face that his eyes would wander over and over again. Watching Isobella, Hydee noticed the look of satisfaction on her arrogant face, then the sneer of contempt that would invariably replace it if her eyes should alight on Hydee. Gasper was her prop throughout the entire evening, and when it was nearing its end and most of the guests were departing, he managed to get her alone while Carlos was in the hall seeing some of his guests away.

'Remember, I shall call for you tomorrow. Is Carlos planning to buy you a car?'

'I can't drive,' she answered, feeling lighthearted at the idea of going out with Gasper the following day. She was not quite sure what her feelings for him were, but she did know that gratitude loomed large.

'You must have a car. I'll teach you to drive.'

'Will Carlos let me have one, do you think?'

'Ask him; it's not an unreasonable request.' He smiled down into her upturned face, an odd expression in his eyes. 'I'll see you tomorrow,' he said again, and moved away from her as Carlos reentered the room.

Hydee was so tired that she merely said a swift good night to her husband and went up to her room, to pace for a few minutes, going over in her mind the events of the evening, recapturing the embarrassments and the pleasures. The latter were provided entirely by Gasper, who had known she would be out of her depth and had come prepared to help her through the ordeal. He had done much to smooth her way, for on the whole she had not been sought out for conversation by many of those present. Arminda had come over for a few words but had soon found a more acceptable companion to talk to; the girl's mother had sniffed as she passed her on her way to socialise with Isobella. As for Carlos, he had been busy, naturally, moving from one group of guests to another, and Hydee could understand his not having much time for her, other than when making the initial introductions. Well, it was all over . . . until Christmas, when there would be another gathering, and this time the relatives would stay for several days. Another ordeal, but she felt sure that Gasper would be there again to help her through it.

She undressed, showered, and wandered from the bathroom into the bedroom. She was just about to pick up her plain cotton nightgown and throw it over her head when, to her amazement, the communicating door opened and Carlos strode in. The angry scowl darkening his face told her instantly that he intended taking her to task over her familiarity with Gasper.

He stopped abruptly, his expression undergoing a change as he saw her naked body. Burning colour flooded into Hydee's cheeks as embarrassment enveloped her, but she could not move to get the nightgown. It was as if she just had to stand there, her hips slender, seductive, her breasts round and virginal above a tiny waist.

'I'm sorry. . . .' Carlos' voice came at last, filtering the deep silence. 'I thought you'd have been in bed. You said you were tired.' Instead of leaving, he came farther into the room, and she did move then, grabbing the nightgown from the back of a chair and

93

getting into it. His eyes watched her every move, and in that moment when he was staring so interestedly, she knew she was in love with him. 'Go away!' she cried. 'Why did you come in here? You've no right!'

He came close, and she stopped, and suddenly she was crying.

'Hydee,' he said, surprising her by his gentleness, 'there's no need to cry.' Taking her hand, he led her to the bed and made her sit down. 'Hydee, don't cry like that,' he commanded. 'Stop it, I say!' He sat down beside her, his strong arm coming about her, and she turned, surprised at his action.

'I'm . . . s-sorry,' she choked, lifting the hem of her nightgown to dry her eyes. 'I suppose it was the . . . the ordeal of tonight.'

'It was an ordeal?' His voice tightened all at once. 'You were happy enough with Gasper,' he reminded her brusquely.

'I needed him, and you must know it.' Carlos avoided making a response to the implied question in her words.

'You're obviously unhappy,' he observed. 'You feel you made a mistake in marrying me?'

Hydee lifted her head; sheer desolation encompassed her at .the knowledge of her hopeless love, and in her misery she said, 'Yes, I *am* beginning to think I made a mistake in marrying you.'

'Already?' He held her from him, his eyes troubled, yet not deeply so, and she wondered if she had been convincing. 'Perhaps the dinner party wasn't a good idea after all.'

'They were all filled with contempt for me and they made no attempt to hide it,' she cried. 'I'm a nobody, but at least I was taught manners. Your family has none!'

Carlos's aristocratic face coloured.

She guessed at his anger while at the same time sensing a reluctance to betray that anger at this time, when she was so distressed. And she recalled her assertion to Gasper that Carlos was kind to her. Yes, she had to admit that up till now he had been kind, giving her full rein with the children, never admonishing her or finding the least fault with her work. He had made her a generous allowance, had told her she must say when she felt she needed a rest from the children. He reminded her that Caterina was quite capable of looking after them temporarily, so there would be no problem if ever she wanted to do a little sightseeing. In any case, he had declared, she must certainly take a trip to Lisbon one day. He had made no mention of accompanying her, and she had not expected him to, but he certainly did not intend to put anything in the way of her having a little pleasure trip now and then.

'The children are tiring and I know it,' he had once said, 'and, therefore, you must tell me whenever you feel like a rest.'

His arm was about her, the strongly comforting scent of his maleness affecting her profoundly, and without thinking, she nestled close against his chest and her hand stole automatically to his shoulder. She thought he stiffened, but when she lifted her face, there was nothing in his expression to denote repugnance; on the contrary, his eyes were compassionate and there was a strange light in them that set her pulses racing in a way she could not understand. His voice was infinitely gentle when at length he spoke, and he drew her even closer, his hand almost tender on her hair.

'You didn't mean it just now when you said you were beginning to regret marrying me?' he said, this time appearing to be a little troubled about it.

'I don't fit in here,' she quavered, a sob in her voice which was the aftermath of tears.

'You wouldn't leave me?'—sharply, even more concern in his voice now.

Hydee hesitated with her answer, thinking of her newly discovered love for him and feeling it would be humanly impossible for her to continue on for long lonely years, carrying the knowledge that there was no possible chance of her love ever being returned. Carlos was looking at her anxiously, and words left her lips that came unthinkingly, for in her unhappiness she scarcely knew what she was saying. 'There's nothing in my life, Carlos. . . .' She broke off as a sob choked the words. 'No hope at all.' She closed her eyes to trap the ready tears that came forth from the heavy cloud at the back of her eyes.

'The children?' Carlos's voice seemed faintly harsh, and yet there was a very odd inflection in it which baffled her and at the same time set her nerves tingling uncontrollably. 'What about them?'

'Yes'—she nodded—'they do fill my daytime hours, and indeed I did assume they'd fill my whole life, but they're not enough. I didn't realise at the time I agreed to marry you that I'd need something else to make my life complete. . . .'

As her thoughts began to clear, she knew she could not continue. The possibility of giving herself away was too strong. It would be an unbearable embarrassment for her if he should ever learn that she had been so foolish as to fall in love with him.

'Something else . . .' Carlos was murmuring so strangely that Hydee searched his face, trying to read his thoughts. 'I ought to have known, to have looked at the situation far more closely, anticipating an eventuality like this.' His facial muscles tightened as a sigh escaped him. Bewildered by his manner, Hydee could only stare, fascinated by the sudden pulsing of a nerve in his throat, the sign of a strong emotion within him. His eyes held hers, disturbing in their intent scrutiny. The silence stretched, brooding, oppressive, and Hydee was suddenly impelled to break it, asking him what he had meant. For answer she received a faintly sardonic smile which served only to baffle her even more.

'Carlos,' she began huskily, 'I—' She stopped abruptly, gasping in surprise as he drew her tightly into his embrace, and before she could even guess at his intention, he was kissing her. For a stunned and disbelieving moment she was robbed of the ability either to move or to think, and she remained passive in his arms while his lips possessed hers, moist and sensuous and thrillingly masterful. It was only when her emotions were stirred that she was galvanised into action, pushing against his chest in an attempt to free herself; but so puny were her efforts against his strength that she gave up, once again passive in his embrace. And soon she found herself reciprocating, her arms sliding up to curl around his neck.

At last he leant away, his eyes inscrutable as they held hers.

'Carlos,' she whispered fervently, 'you kissed me. . . .'

'Yes, dear.' A smile softened the hard outline of his mouth. 'I kissed you because I wanted to.'

'Because you wanted to. . . .' Her heart was leaping, blood surging into it from every part of her body. It couldn't be true, she was telling herself one moment, yet the next moment she was thrilling to the knowledge that it *was* true. Hydee dared not presume that Carlos had suddenly fallen in love with her, but undoubtedly he found something attractive in her; he must have done, to have held her like that and kissed her so tenderly and yet with an ardour that betrayed his need of her. Dazed, yet with a tentative rapture stealing along her nerves, she waited for him to speak again, but instead he drew her into his arms and sought her lips. He kissed her gently at first but then with an increasing passion that had the instant effect of heightening her own emotions, and she clung to him, all her love pouring out in her reciprocation of his kisses. She parted her lips readily at the insistence of his, thrilling to the male roughness of his tongue against the tender flesh within her mouth.

Her temperature seemed to be rising with the increase of his ardour as his kisses became more sensuous, more passionate, his lips moving from her mouth to the tender curve of her throat, moist and tempting against her soft white skin. His lips found hers again after their explorations, and a spasm of ecstasy shot through her at the sensory effect of his tongue caressing hers. Her strong young arms encircled his neck; she thrilled to the knowledge of his uneven breathing when she caressed his nape, to the little shock he sustained when her fingers played lightly with a sensitive place behind his ear.

As his ardour grew, his lean hands caressed; he managed somehow to reach her breast in spite of the protection of the nightdress, gently cupping it as if enjoying its weight within his palm. As quivers of longing rippled through Hydee's whole body, she heard him whisper hoarsely, 'Hydee . . . my wife. . . .' That was all. She submitted without protest when he took the nightdress away, colouring delicately yet moving close to find comfort against him. He laid her on the bed and went out, returning ten minutes later clad in a dressing gown. Hydee lay supine and content, watching him take it off.

'I love you, Carlos,' she said, but it was a whisper not meant for her husband's hearing.

Chapter Nine

It was a soft and gentle morning with not a cloud to stain the ice-blue crystal of the sky. The sun's slanting rays were already diffusing an autumnal warmth and brilliance over the drowsy landscape.

Hydee had been up since first light and was wandering about the now familiar grounds, stopping every so often to admire a dew-flushed rose or other exotic, sweetly perfumed flower. The fountain shot its spray into the air, snatching colour from the sun. Beside an ornamental pool two white marble statues of Greek gods looked down enigmatically from their high pedestals, at the foot of which three peacocks preened themselves. Hydee took this stroll every morning, savouring the solitude, the peace and purity of the dawn. Her thoughts would wander always, flitting about from one thing to another, but now she was recalling vividly the events of last night. They had come so unexpectedly. Had he felt sorry for her? she had asked herself after it was all over and she was lying by his side, content to be there even though she knew he did not love her. She decided that it was not pity that had led him to make love to her, but desire pure and simple. And he had derived such pleasure from her body that she had no doubts about his wanting to come to her again. That he might be in love with Arminda was a possibility looming large on her horizon, but Hydee did not intend to let it trouble her. She was happier than she had been this time yesterday; she had the children in the daytime and the fulfilment of her love to look forward to at night. Added to this was the cherished hope that, one day—perhaps in the far distant future—Carlos would come to love her as deeply as she loved him. Inevitably she pondered about her love for Noel, and realised that what she had felt for him was weak and insipid in comparison to the depth of her love for her husband.

Her thoughts reverting to last night, she wondered why she'd had no instinct to resist, aware as she was that Carlos did not love her. She ought to have had a feeling of shame, of being unclean, almost, because she had such high ideals about love and marriage and the spiritual oneness of a union based on love. She'd had no doubts about being swept to the realms of rapture, because she knew instinctively that Carlos would prove to be the perfect lover, experienced, skilled in the art of lovemaking. But how long would physical pleasure satisfy her if there were no subsequent feeling of permanency and depth, of absolute confidence and the tender warmth of love's after-play?

None of this had come to her as Carlos prepared to lie down beside her. On the contrary, she had wanted him desperately, and in the craving for the fulfilment of her own love there had been no place for doubts and questions and the conjectures that were now running through her mind. She threw them off, remembering that whatever the circumstances created by this new and unexpected relationship, she was far happier than she had been before.

And with this in mind she wandered on, stopping by a scented bush to stare back at the Palacio, occupying its dramatic setting on the spur of the hill overlooking the Douro Valley, its glorious and extensive grounds alive with colour from geraniums and lilies and pink-flushed roses. Magnolias and bougainvillaeas grew parallel to a hedge of brilliant red hibiscus, and in another part of the garden a bed of dahlias shone like purest gold in the morning sunshine. From this vantage point Hydee could see the extensive vinyards of the *quinta*, terraces cut into the steep sides of the valley, but all was silent now, for the vintage was over, the vines resting, the whole aspect a little lost and forlorn after the tremendous activity of the vintage.

Glancing at her watch, Hydee gave a little start of disbelief and hurried back to the house. Ramos and Luisa were having a tussle in the nursery when she entered, and she stood for a moment watching them.

'Mama!' exclaimed Ramos, running to her; he grasped her hand, putting it to his cheek in a gesture of affection. 'Where have you been? We're hungry!'

Within half an hour she had them both washed

and dressed and entering the breakfast salon, where their father was already waiting.

It was natural that Hydee should expect to experience some embarrassment on meeting Carlos, but she scarcely felt it because the presence of the children diverted her husband's thoughts from last night and the only sign that he remembered was an inquiry, spoken in a casual tone, as to how she had slept.

And even then her brief reply was interrupted by Ramos and Luisa saying in unison, 'Good morning, Papa! Is breakfast ready? Because we're hungry,' added Ramos, hitching himself up into a chair.

His father regarded him sternly. 'Have you forgotten your manners, Ramos?' he inquired with a slight inclination of his head towards where Luisa was standing, looking rather superior as she waited to see what her brother would do.

'She can get up by herself,' growled Ramos, sending her a frowning look.

'Undoubtedly she can,' agreed Carlos. 'Nevertheless, you will use your manners and see her to her chair.'

Drawing a long loud breath, Ramos obeyed, bringing out a chair for his sister and waiting until she was seated in it before returning to his own. How very nicely they were being brought up, thought Hydee, feeling proud and privileged to be their stepmother.

After Carlos had performed a similar courtesy for his wife, they all had breakfast, a happy, normal family, the children being allowed a certain amount of freedom to talk, both to each other and to their parents.

'Casco will be ready to take you to school,' Hydee

prompted when Luisa began to dally with her food. 'Don't you want any more?'

'Yes, I want it all.'

Another wait and then, from Carlos, 'I'm sure, Luisa, that you've had enough. Come on—move, or you'll be late for school.'

Hydee stood on the Palacio steps and waved to them as the car moved off the forecourt, leaving the impressive precincts of the Palacio as it rolled down the mile-long drive towards the road.

Carlos had already gone off, saying he would not be home until late in the afternoon, and Hydee went to the nursery to pick up the children's dirty clothes in readiness for Ana, who would be coming to collect them. Less than half an hour later she heard Gasper's car crunch to a stop on the gravel; going to the window, she waved and smiled, calling down to him that she would be there directly.

He drove her along leafy lanes for less than five miles before turning into an entrance equally as imposing as that of the Palacio de Manrique.

'Do all Carlos's relatives live in palaces like this?' she inquired when, through the trees, she saw the eighteenth-century country palace with its tall Moorish-type pillars supporting a high balcony that ran the entire length of the front façade of the house.

'Not all,' he laughed, 'but most of us do. The aunts are rather impoverished, being widows, but although they might be reduced in circumstances, it's certainly not affected their arrogance.'

So I noticed, thought Hydee silently.

Gasper was speaking again, this time about the house. 'It occupies an ancient river terrace,' he explained, and as they got out of the car he pointed to the river, which flowed slowly beside the *palacio*.

'It gives it extraordinary charm,' enthused Hydee, standing motionless in appreciation as her eyes wandered all around the formal gardens with their statuary and *azulejos,* their several waterfalls and boundless expanses of smooth green lawn and shrubberies and parterres. 'It's really lovely, Gasper.' She turned to look up at him with that limpid quality in her eyes that had attracted him from the first, although of course Hydee did not know it. 'You're the owner? You have no parents?'

He shook his head. 'I've been the owner since I was twelve.'

'Twelve?' Her lovely eyes were pained as she asked how that came to be.

'Mother died when I was three and Father when I was twelve. Carlos kept an eye on the estate until I came of age—he's ten years older than I, and even at the age of twenty-two he was businesslike and capable. His estate came to him when he was twenty-five.' They were standing close together on the white marble forecourt; he looked down at her with a rueful expression on his handsome face. 'Thank your lucky stars that his mother is no more. She was worse than her daughter; she considered the family of Manrique to be so exalted that she expected everyone to bow down to her.'

Hydee stared. 'You're not serious?'

'Every servant had to incline his or her head when meeting up with the marquesa. Yet her husband was so different—proud and arrogant, of course, but certainly not bloated with his own superiority in the way his wife was. I hated her and she me.'

'What about Carlos?' began Hydee curiously. 'How did he get along with her?'

'Not very well. However, she was very taken with

his wife—thought the sun shone out of her, which only goes to show, because Eunice was not only unfaithful, but she turned out to be a bad mother.'

'Really? I gathered that Ramos and Luisa led rather a restricted life when their mother was alive.'

'Yes, but strict discipline cannot take the place of love. Luckily, Carlos was always there to provide that. And although he's less rigid in his discipline than any other parent in our family, there are limits to his tolerence, and Ramos and Luisa know that if they go beyond them they're in trouble.'

Hydee could well imagine that, and she hoped she would never be a witness to Carlos' anger if ever it should be directed against one of his children.

To Hydee's surprise, Carlos was at home when she arrived back after a most pleasant few hours. Gasper had taken her on an extensive tour, first to the gallery of paintings, then from room to room, the entire aspect of the palace giving the impression of wealth and graceful living. They strolled in the garden while waiting for lunch to be served on the terrace, and, profoundly appreciative of a beauty she had never dreamed could exist, Hydee often gasped audibly at what she saw.

When, after dropping her at her home, Gasper invited her to come again, her acceptance came eagerly and naturally as she said she would love to come anytime he wanted her to. 'And thank you for a lovely few hours today, Gasper.'

'No need for thanks, my dear.' Serious and somewhat intense as his eyes met hers, Gasper added softly, 'I have never had more pleasant company, Hydee. You're charming and graceful . . . and desirable.'

Colouring delicately, Hydee watched his expression close, yet the next moment he was as carefree as ever as he slid into the car, lifted a hand in salute, then crunched away over the gravel, to gain speed on reaching the smoother surface of the tree-shaded drive leading to the road.

For a long moment Hydee stood there, still and silent as she watched the dust rise in the wake of the car.

It was as she turned to the house that she saw Carlos at the window of the sitting room, and her heart gave a little lurch because she knew full well that he would not be at all pleased that she had been with his cousin. However, deciding there was nothing to be gained by meeting trouble halfway, she greeted him with a happy smile and asked why he was earlier than he had said.

Carlos pointedly ignored her question. 'You've been with Gasper all day?' he asked in a voice that chilled her to the bone.

'Not all day,' she answered, automatically glancing at the French marble clock on the mantelshelf. 'Were you home for lunch?'

'I was'—briefly and with the intention of disconcerting her still more.

'I'm sorry.' Her face broke into a difficult smile as instinctively she attempted to assuage his anger. 'When you went out this morning, you said you wouldn't be back for lunch.'

Carlos regarded her darkly from his superior height. 'The arrangement with Gasper was made last night obviously?'

'Yes; he offered to take me to see his home.' The colour was swiftly leaving her face. 'You're not pleased that I went with him?'

'You are fully aware that I'm not pleased.' The wrathful intensity of his stare sent tremors of apprehension running along her spine, and she half-turned, an involuntary movement born of the natural instinct to escape. 'You know my opinion of him; I've mentioned that he's a flirt, a philanderer.'

'Yes, but he would never say anything out of place to me, Carlos,' she said, nervous tension sharpening her tone. 'After all, he's my cousin-in-law, so surely you don't mind our being friends?'

His eyes remained dark and wrathful, and there was no relaxing of the tight uncompromising line of his mouth while she was speaking to him in a pleading voice.

'You went off with him without even mentioning to me that you'd made this date—'

'It wasn't a date,' she broke in swiftly. 'It—'

'What was it, then? Are we to begin splitting hairs?'

'It . . . it was merely an invitation which he extended from a sense of duty.'

A sneer curled her husband's mouth. 'I do not approve of Gasper—or his peculiar sense of "duty," as you so delicately describe it.' He paused as if affording her the opportunity to respond, but the little lump that had risen in her throat prevented speech. She was desolate at the change in Carlos after the intimacy of last night. She had not supposed that their new relationship would produce any swift and dramatic change in him, but neither had she envisaged his being like this—standing there in judgement, tall and forbidding and adopting a magisterial attitude, as if she were nothing more than the nanny she had first expected to be.

'I like Gasper,' she just had to say, because it was

108

true, and even if he was a flirt and a philanderer, she could not see how this would ever affect her. 'He's jolly, and amiable—'

'Too jolly and amiable,' interposed Carlos grittingly. 'There's already a good deal of talk going on regarding our marriage, and I don't intend to encourage additional gossip by allowing you to run around with a man whose moral character is well-known to all the family.'

'Talk?' she repeated, bypassing all the rest, and staring at him questioningly. 'What kind of talk?'

'Doreen was stupid enough to tell my sister the circumstances leading up to our marriage—'

'And Isobella repeated them to you?'

'Not to me, but to every other member of the family.' He stopped, his mouth compressing angrily. 'She's said something to you, no doubt?'

'I'd rather not talk about it,' returned Hydee in a taut voice that was bound to rivet his attention.

'So she *has* been talking to you.' Anger seemed to have left him, but his brow was darkened by a frown. 'I'd like to know what she said.' Implacable the tone, demanding and masterful. Hydee's hesitation was only temporary, for she knew that obedience to his wishes must override her reluctance to disclose what Isobella had said to her.

'She was disappointed that you didn't marry Arminda.'

The dark, foreign eyes narrowed to mere slits. 'She actually told you that?' There was incredulity in his tone, but Hydee knew he believed her when she said yes, Isobella had in fact told her that.

'I can understand her disappointment but not her deliberate vindictiveness,' Hydee added on a bitter note.

'What else did she say?' demanded Carlos, ignoring what Hydee had just said.

'She knows it's a marriage of convenience.'

'She does?' with an arrogant lift of his brows. 'Well, she'll know differently if, in the not-too-distant future, you have a child.'

A child. . . . Yes, it was natural that he should expect a child to come eventually.

'You would like us to have a child?' A wave of pure happiness swept over her at the idea of having Carlos's child.

'Of course. Wouldn't you?' His eyes were actually smiling now, and her happiness increased.

'Yes, Carlos, I would like that very much.'

The smile reached his lips. 'Luisa and Ramos would like it, too. I rather think that Luisa would completely lose interest in her dolls.' All his ill-humour had evaporated, and there seemed to be a hint of tenderness in the glance he gave her before saying, 'Don't go out with Gasper again, Hydee. It would displease and anger me, and I'm sure you wouldn't want that.'

She looked up into his stern, set face, aware of the change in the atmosphere as she hesitated before answering him. 'I don't want to displease you, Carlos, but Gasper has become important in my life—'

'Important?' he snapped, eyes kindling.

'As a friend. Oh, Carlos, I did tell you I needed him, and it's true! Please don't forbid me his company. You must know you can trust me!'

'I don't trust Gasper,' was his quietly spoken rejoinder, 'and, therefore, I am asking you not to go out with him again.'

She bit her lip, aware of her husband's mastery,

aware that it would be far more comfortable to obey him without argument or pleading, yet she found herself saying, 'There's no harm in our friendship, Carlos.'

'Except that gossip is bound to result, and as I have just said, I will not tolerate it.' His voice was implacable, edged with finality, and so it was no surprise to Hydee when he turned on his heel and left her there alone, her misted eyes fixed on the closed door for a long moment after he had gone.

Chapter Ten

Night had fallen softly to clothe the drowsy land-scape with a deep purple sheen, increased in its intensity by the vibrance of the sky. On the whisper-ing eddies of the breeze there floated the tang of herbs, while high above, in the star-misted dome of the heavens, clouds in moonglow appeared like lace, spun in silver by some fairy hand.

Hydee's mouth curved in a contented smile as she stood by the fountain, her dreamy eyes scanning the exotic scene around her. She and Carlos had dined and had been about to go to the green-and-gold salon for their coffee when he had been called to the telephone, and as he had come back to warn her that the call would take some time, she had said she would wander out to the garden and wait for him there.

Strolling over to a rustic seat she sat down, her mind filled with the new relationship that had come to her and Carlos. Even now, after almost a week, it seemed a miracle that he wanted her in that way. Yet he did; she had no doubts whatsoever as to the pleasure he derived from her body, just as she derived pleasure from his. But she was always aware that he did not love her, and now and then a ruthless stab of jealousy would inflict its pain because of Arminda and Carlos's feelings for her. Twice Hydee had been urged by some force beyond her control to mention the girl, to put a casual question. On both occasions he had answered curtly and she was unhappily conscious of being snubbed. Gasper had phoned twice, the second time to try to pin her down to a definite date. Hydee had deftly managed to avoid being pressed to make a decision, but although for the present she was obeying her husband's order, it was with a feeling of indignation at not being able to have a little freedom to do what she wanted to do. After all, Carlos was out for most of the day, or in his study, and being left to her own devices, Hydee would very much have liked to be able to enjoy Gasper's company without any fear of stirring her husband's anger.

However, for the present Hydee was content to let things sail along as they were, her early mornings and afternoons taken up with the children and her evenings and nights spent most pleasantly with her husband. And, to add to her happiness, she had received a letter from Ellie saying that she and Ray were getting married two days before Christmas and asking tentatively if it would be all right for them to come over for their honeymoon. Hydee had shown her husband the letter, watching his handsome face anxiously, relieved when, on handing it back to her, he had produced a smile.

'A honeymoon couple joining us for Christmas. That will be something new. Yes, Hydee, let them come, by all means. We have a houseful, so two more won't upset either the menu or the accommodation arrangements.'

Hydee had warmed to Carlos even more then, happy to know he did not intend to despise her friends. What the rest of the family would have to say was something else altogether, she mused with a grimace, but as she cared not one jot for their opinion, she managed without difficulty to thrust the matter from her mind.

Suddenly her heart caught, and sheer joy spread through her being as she saw the tall silhouette of her husband's figure swinging along the path as if he walked on air.

'Sorry to leave you all that time,' he apologised gracefully as he stood there, towering above her so that she felt small and insignificant, and very much under his domination. But in her lovely eyes there was eagerness and excitement, and her whole body felt as if it floated on a warm silken carpet of pure magic. As if fully aware of her heightened emotions, Carlos reached down to take her hand in a firm and masterful grip that brought her to her feet and drew her close. His other hand spread its long lean fingers from her waist to the small of her back, lingering awhile to let her feel its strength and its warmth before travelling in a slow, sensuous motion to her bare shoulder, tracing a line along the tender curve of her throat to tease with experienced finesse the sensitive places behind her ear and along the nape of her neck. His caresses were gentle, sophisticated, yet calculated to arouse her desires, as were the kisses he rained on her temples, her eyes, her eager, moistly glowing lips.

Her tremors of rapture very soon made him realise that this was no place to be, and he silently led her back to the house, his arm about her waist, his fingers sensuously probing and kneading, enticing her readiness for him even before they reached their suite. Once there, he left her, to return ten minutes or so later when the pervasive scent of his newly applied after-shave apprised Hydee of the fact that, like her, he had showered. He wore a blue silk dressing gown loosely fastened by a cord; Hydee's négligé covered a dainty see-through nightdress bought a couple of days ago and of a kind she had never worn before. She made no demur when her husband slid the négligé from her shoulders and threw it onto a chair, and even her reaction to his removal of the nightdress was no more than a little halfhearted protest which was immediately smothered by his kiss. But she coloured delicately and Carlos seemed amused that she could blush as easily as she had a week ago.

'You're very lovely when you blush like that.' No smile, but an undertone of fondness in his voice which eradicated the impression of severity. 'I'm your husband, so there's no need for embarrassment, surely?'

'It hasn't been long yet, Carlos,' she returned

softly, her eyes watching his make their now familiar exploration of her body. It was a cool appraisal at first, but it warmed ardently as he assessed the potential delight of her curves. With an overpowering strength, he drew her into an embrace which brought her naked body to his. Her own need pulsated to life as his lips possessed hers, hard and demanding and insistent with primitive mastery.

The feel of his hand on her breast, fingers teasing the nipple to the hardness of desire, sent ecstasy quivering through her veins. All embarrassment dissolved by her desperate need of him, Hydee slid a finger into the loop of the cord and let his dressing gown come open. She strained against the rippling muscles of his nakedness, all her love outflowing, fused with the abandon of her primitive desire to give herself to him in tenderness and sweet surrender. And when at last she did surrender, her reward was the flow of a drenching rapture that swept her to the edge of paradise . . . and beyond.

The following two weeks passed happily for Hydee, who, on asking Carlos if she could learn to drive, was immediately provided with an instructor from the driving school in the nearest town. She remembered that Gasper had promised to teach her, but she naturally made no mention of this to Carlos.

Gasper rang again when Carlos was out and asked if he could call for her and give her a lunch at his home. She made an excuse, but still resented having to forfeit the harmless pleasure of his bright company. During the fortnight the children had a four-day break from school, and that, too, had been a happy interlude for Hydee. Apart from the time taken up by her driving lessons, she was with them throughout the entire day. They swam in the pool, played ball on the lawn and went for rambles into the surrounding countryside.

Then, right out of the blue, Carlos said he was going to London on business. Hydee would very much have liked to go with him, and for some time considered making a tentative suggestion, bearing in mind what Carlos had said about Caterina being competent to look after the children. However, she reluctantly concluded that if Carlos had wanted her with him he would have been the one to make the suggestion. He did not do so, and on Thursday morning very early he left, being driven to the airport by Geraldo, one of the chauffeurs.

'When will you be back?' Hydee asked, having risen early so as to have her breakfast with him.

'I can't say for sure, Hydee. My business might take a week or, on the other hand, it could be concluded in a few days. I'll phone you from my hotel.' His smile was amicable enough but lacked the near-tenderness to which Hydee had recently become used. His general attitude, too, seemed to be offhand, and a chill settled on her heart. It was absurd, she knew, to feel like this, because her husband's manner in all probability resulted from his having to be off extra early to catch the plane, and perhaps from his concentration on the business which necessitated his travelling to London. She had made tentative and subtle inquiries about this business, but refrained after she had been almost snubbed. She could not understand why he was so reticent about it, especially in light of the new relationship which now existed between them. She had become a proper wife physically, so why not his confidante and friend as well?

Such a relationship might come eventually, she told herself as she stood at the head of the white marble steps and waved as the car drew off the forecourt. Then she felt flat, drained, and although she gave herself a mental shake, she still felt depressed when she saw the children off to school two hours later.

At half-past ten her driving instructor arrived and the lesson made a break from the sort of nerve-twisting tension that was beginning to assail her. She did not know what was the matter with her but was relieved to learn that her driving had not suffered.

'You're doing very well indeed,' praised the man, Jorge, speaking good but broken English. 'It is a long time since I had such an apt pupil.'

He left her at the door, and the tension returned immediately. She would phone Gasper, she decided on the spur of the moment, just for a chat, that was all.

'Hello!' he greeted her eagerly. 'How are things with my beautiful cousin-in-law?'

'Not too bad,' she began, then wished she had forced a little more brightness into her voice.

'Sounds somewhat suspicious,' he said, gravity replacing the previous jocular tone of his voice. 'Something wrong?'

'Nothing at all, Gasper. How are you these days?'

'Great, as always. But we were talking about you. You've been putting me off all the time, so I conclude you've had orders not to cultivate me. Right?'

'Carlos says you're a flirt, and it's true.'

'Admitted, but he knows I wouldn't flirt with his wife.' A slight pause ensued. 'Where is he now? In his study with his nose to his books?'

'He went off to London this morning early.'

'He did!' Silence, so prolonged that Hydee wondered if they'd been cut off.

'Are you still there, Gasper?' she said. ·

'Yes, of course. London, eh? Did he say why he was going there?'

'On business.' Nerves twisted in Hydee's stomach as if she knew instinctively that there must be a very good reason for the way she had been feeling this morning. 'Why are you acting so strangely?' she just had to inquire.

'Strangely?' Hydee had the impression he was pulling himself together. 'That's a funny thing to say, Hydee. Why on earth should I act strangely?' And when she offered no answer, he asked if he could come over and take her to lunch, either to his own house or to a restaurant.

She hesitated, but only for a few seconds. She was far too depressed to refuse the opportunity of being cheered up.

'All right, Gasper.' She glanced at her wristwatch. 'It's a quarter to twelve now. What time should I expect you?'

'I'll be on my way in a couple of minutes.' The line went dead. Hydee stared at the receiver for a long moment before replacing it on its rest. Gasper's attitude *had* been strange, no matter how he denied it, she thought, making her way up the beautiful balustraded staircase to her bedroom on the wide semicircular corridor at the top of it.

She looked especially charming when she met

Gasper in the cool, marble-floored hallway with its fluted pillars and the crest embellishing the wide arch through which could be seen the broad and sweeping stairway.

Gasper stood there, waiting for Bento to disappear before he said, a soft whistle having already issued from his lips, 'You're a real beauty if ever there was one! Hydee, why didn't I meet you before that lucky and unappreciative cousin of mine?'

Having decided to assume a light and casual front, Hydee forced herself to laugh. 'You're incorrigible, Gasper. But keep your flirting for those who enjoy it. I'm a married woman and very conscious of the fact.'

'Married?' with a lift of one noble eyebrow. 'In name only—is that a marriage?'

She coloured but turned at the same time, embarrassed, and wished there was some casual way of informing him of the new relationship she had with her husband.

'Shall we go into the salon and have a drink?' she suggested, moving away even before he could speak.

They sat together on a couch, Hydee with a long cooling drink and Gasper with something stronger, their conversation light and general even though the questions which both wished to ask hovered on the edge of their minds.

At last Gasper said, regarding Hydee intently as he lifted his glass to sip its sparkling amber contents, 'So Carlos went off to London this morning, did he? And how long is he to be away?'

'It could be a week, but probably a little less.'

A strange silence prevailed, and when she saw that Gasper was deep in thought and not ready to comment, Hydee just had to ask, 'Why did you sound so strange on the phone, Gasper?— no, don't deny it again, please.' She lifted a hand to strengthen the plea. 'Right at the beginning there was an understanding between you and me that frankness would be important in our friendship. Well, Gasper, you are not at present being frank with me. Just what are you trying to hide?'

'Are you omniscient?' he demanded, faintly angry.

Hydee's smile was slow and thin. 'I don't have to possess abnormal powers of observation to see that you know something about Carlos's visit to London that I don't.'

Gasper watched her move her glass so that the ice tinkled on its sides and said frowningly, 'I feel that the frankness you speak of might not be either desirable or in any way advantageous under the circumstances.'

It was Hydee's turn to frown. She tried to dismiss the matter, but her curiosity was too strong. Besides, that nagging tension remained with her, increased by Gasper's manner, gnawing into her consciousness to form a persistent irritation to her nerves. She *must* know what he was keeping from her! She would not allow him any peace until he submitted a forthright answer to her question.

'You're making things even worse,' she pointed out quietly.

'Because I have my back to the wall,' he retorted, and again she detected a hint of anger in his voice.

'It's very plain that Carlos's visit to London has some kind of mystery surrounding it.'

'That's not so,' he immediately denied. 'Carlos

often goes to London on business—' He broke off as Bento knocked quietly and entered, with the information that Dona Isobella had called.

'Didn't you tell her that Dom Carlos is away?' said Hydee with a frown.

'I did, senhora, but she then said she would like to see you.'

'What now?' said Gasper, exchanging glances with Hydee. 'Not a friendly, affectionate sisterly visit, I'll be bound.' He seemed troubled, she thought, which only served to add to her puzzlement and disturbance of mind.

'I could very well have done without a visit from my haughty sister-in-law at this particular time,' she sighed, voicing her thoughts aloud.

'Shall I show her in, senhora?' Bento's voice sounded a trifle pained and, as usual, stolid. Why did he make her feel so inferior? wondered Hydee with a swift spurt of anger. Would the time ever come when he would treat her as an equal with her exalted husband and his equally high-bred relatives?

'I am in, Bento, thank you.' The clipped and arrogant voice actually startled Hydee, because she had not expected her sister-in-law to take it upon herself to come in without first having Hydee's invitation conveyed to her via the butler. Isobella stood just inside the door, her dark unfathomable eyes moving slowly from one occupant of the couch to the other before Gasper, remembering his manners, rose reluctantly, undisguised dislike imprinted on his face.

'Good day to you, Isobella. I trust you and your family are in good health?'

'If you mean Pedro and his father, then, yes, Gasper, they are both in excellent health.'

So formal and stilted! Hydee felt that Isobella would have better fitted into a society existing a hundred years ago.

'Do sit down,' she invited, rising from the couch to tug at an ornate bell rope. 'What refreshments can I get you?'

'None, thank you,' answered Isobella tersely, her eyes wandering to Gasper, standing there, tall and aristocratic and almost as good-looking as Carlos. 'It would seem I'm interrupting your little tête-à-tête, so I won't stay.'

'But Bento said you wanted to see me,' put in Hydee as Isobella turned towards the door through which she had only just entered. 'What is it?' Cool the voice, composed the manner, but underneath it all Hydee was trembling, for she felt herself to be vulnerable to great danger, knew a sensation of being poised on the edge of a precipice over which it would take no more than a puff of wind to make her fall. In her imagination she could see Isobella talking to Carlos, then very casually letting it drop that she had called and Gasper had been there sitting close to Hydee on the sofa. Yes, Hydee knew by the woman's expression what was running through her mind, what plans she was making to bring about her hated sister-in-law's downfall. Carlos's first wife was fond of other men, had been unfaithful, so it was logical to assume that Carlos would be furious about Gasper being there, especially as he had told Hydee not to cultivate his friendship.

'It was nothing really important—' began Isobella, when her cousin interrupted her.

'Nothing you can speak of before me, Isobella? Do you want me to remove myself so that you can talk to Hydee in private?' Although he had asked the question, Hydee had the impression that the last thing he wanted was to leave them alone together.

'No, don't go, Gasper. As I said, it was nothing of any real importance.' Suddenly her whole manner changed and she smiled in the most disarming way. 'I *will* have a drink, after all, Hydee,' she said, moving over to a chair and sitting down. Her eyes sought Hydee's figure, sweeping over it to take in the exceptionally pretty dress she wore—a full-skirted dress of pale blue cotton with a tight-fitting bodice and dainty trimmings of narrow brown lace on the edge of the short sleeves and on the hemline. 'So, Carlos is in London,' she murmured softly. 'I wonder if he'll run across Arminda.'

'Arminda?' repeated Hydee, eyes sliding to Gasper, and narrowing as he glanced away, refusing to meet her gaze.

'Yes.' Isobella smiled as she leant back and crossed her shapely legs. 'She went over a couple of days ago. She has an aunt living in Mayfair whom she visits two or three times a year.'

A chill passed over Hydee's body, spreading into her heart to slow its beating, and for one wild moment of sheer misery she thought that if she were dying she would not mind. For with vivid perception she now understood her husband's refusal to tell her what his business was. And then there was Gasper's attitude, his swiftly curtailed exclamation on being told that Carlos was flying to London that day.

Hydee looked towards the door with a swift frown as Felix, a young manservant working under Bento, entered in answer to Hydee's summons.

'What will you have, Isobella?' she asked, but Gasper spoke at the same time, actually telling Felix to leave the room. 'What . . . ?' Hydee stared blankly at him, noting the arrogance and the hard, steely expression which reminded her of Carlos in one of his less attractive moods.

'I think you had better leave, Isobella. You've done what you came for, although you chose to go a long way about it, just for effect I guess, knowing you as well as I do.'

'I don't know what you're talking about, Gasper!' Isobella said something in Portuguese, and Hydee saw Gasper's teeth clamp together and his fists close at his sides. He moved closer to where his cousin sat and stood over her, a menacing figure, his handsome face dark with fury.

'I told you to leave,' he gritted. 'You called here for the specific purpose of letting Hydee know that Arminda's in London, because you want to hurt her! Also, when you saw my car *out there* you were curious as to what was going on *in here!* Well, now you know—and you'll put your own interpretation on it! But I warn you, Isobella, be very careful about blackening Hydee's name, either with her husband or with any other members of our family! I can retaliate, remember—*remember?'* The words were deliberate, with an undertone of contempt. 'Yes,' he sneered as the blood rushed to Isobella's face, a betrayal of her guilt over some indiscretion obviously known to her cousin, 'I see that you do remember! So think before you let that venomous tongue of yours get you into trouble. And now,' he added finally, 'you can go!'

'You'll allow Gasper to order me out of my own brother's home?' The question was thrown at Hydee, who could only stand there trembling from head to foot, the icy chill of wounded pride spreading through the hollowness within her. 'Well?' snapped her sister-in-law, her mouth beginning to twist convulsively, the result of an all-consuming fury that seemed to pervade the entire atmosphere of the room.

'Your brother's home?' from Gasper when Hydee still remained dumb. 'I'm ordering you out of *Hydee's* home. Now, go before I forget I'm a gentleman!' He was at the door; Isobella rose with difficulty but marched from the room with head held high, the imprint of hate and arrogance in every step she took.

Although the atmosphere in the salon seemed lighter and fresher when Isobella had gone, the two who were left found difficulty in breaking the long silence which followed the slamming of the door. But at last Gasper spoke, moving to put a comforting arm around Hydee's drooping shoulders.

'Try to forget her, Hydee, dear. She's just about the worst of a family I am certainly not proud to belong to.'

Eyes misted with tears were lifted to his face. Hydee saw his expression change and answered his question before he had time to ask it. 'Yes, Gasper, I love him. It was bound to happen. I know that now.'

'What a mess! And him caring for . . .' He stopped, but Hydee finished for him, '. . . Arminda. They planned to be together didn't they?' No answer and she went on, 'You knew Arminda was going to London, didn't you?'

'Yes,' he replied after a fleeting pause, 'I did.'

'And it was a shock when you knew Carlos was there, too.'

'It was a surprise, certainly.' He looked down into her face, and before Hydee had time to avoid what she realised was coming, Gasper had bent his head to kiss her full on the lips.

It was at that moment that Isobella returned,

throwing open the door and saying coldly, 'I left my handbag. . . .' Her tall figure seemed to dominate the room as Hydee and Gasper fell apart, not with any special haste, because it was too late for that. 'So I wasn't mistaken when I suspected an affair,' sneered the woman triumphantly. 'Oh, well, as Carlos is also having an affair, I don't really blame you—'

'Carlos is not having an affair!' seethed Hydee, sparks of fury igniting in her eyes. 'You're just trying to make mischief, Isobella, because Carlos didn't marry the girl you wanted him to! But it's wicked to say he's having an affair with Arminda, because you know it's all lies!' Control was almost gone, but by a supreme effort Hydee recovered, and her head was lifted with pride, her shoulders squared, as she looked into the arrogantly hostile face of the woman who had hated her from the moment of their first meeting—no, even before that, before they had even met.

Slowly Isobella moved to the chair on which she had left her bag. 'It's natural that you should try to convince yourself that what I've said is untrue,' she sneered, 'but if you don't believe *me*, ask Gasper. He's so clever, poking into the private affairs of every one of us so that he always has something to hold over us. Yes, ask him about Carlos and Arminda. They became lovers almost as soon as Arminda and her mother came to live in this district.'

'Isobella,' Gasper hissed through his teeth, 'will you take your bag and get out of here?'

The door closed more quietly this time. Hydee turned to Gasper and said on a note of dull resignation, 'What she said is true, isn't it? Carlos and

Arminda *are* lovers. They wouldn't be together in London now if they weren't.'

The frown that creased his forehead answered her, and something sharp and cruel slashed its way into her heart, coiling around it like a poisonous snake. Only now did she fully realise that, despite all that had occurred, all that looked black against her husband, deep within her she had clung to a ray of hope and trust. For although she had admitted that Carlos cared for Arminda, Hydee had been unable to accept that he was her lover.

'I'm sorry, Hydee,' said Gasper hoarsely. 'I'd have done anything for this not to have happened. Isobella . . . she's poison! I've said so before, and I say it again!'

'I'd have found out sometime,' said Hydee with a little choking sob. She could not help thinking about her new relationship with Carlos, a relationship which she had cherished with tenderness and the hope that, one day in the future, he would return her love.

And now there was no hope for her, no future, because she was unable to see herself living with a man who had a mistress as well as a wife. Yet what about the children? How could she leave them now that they had grown to love her?

'Hydee. . . .' Gasper's voice recalled her and she looked at him through eyes shadowed by unhappiness. 'What can I say, Hydee, dear? How can I help?'

A bitter smile twisted her mouth. 'No one can help, Gasper,' she answered gently. 'My friend Ellie warned me I was making a mistake, and now I know she was right. I wouldn't listen because I thought I knew what I wanted. It never occurred to me that I'd fall in love with my husband. . . . It all seemed so nicely cut and dried in the beginning, but fate stepped in, and now where are all my well-laid plans and resolutions?'

'Try not to be bitter, Hydee. It will destroy you swifter than anything I know. Look at Isobella—she's bitter over Carlos's choice of a wife, and the bitterness is eating into her very soul.'

'She's still hoping that Arminda will one day become Carlos's wife.' A pause, but Gasper did not speak. He had pulled the bell rope and Hydee realised he felt the need of a drink—a strong one, probably. 'Perhaps she'll achieve her ambition—I don't know. I can't even think clearly.'

'It's understandable.'

'Are you taking me out to lunch?' She scarcely knew why she said that; all she did know was that a certain lethargy was slowly creeping over her, soothing her in some unbelievable way, almost numbing her mind to the pain inflicted on it within the last few minutes. Reaction would undoubtedly set in, she knew, but for the present she wanted only to get away from here, away from the Palacio and especially this particular room, which she felt she would always hate.

'Shall we have it at my home, or would you rather go to a restaurant?'

She considered a moment. 'At your home, I think, Gasper.'

'You do know that Carlos won't approve?' Gasper watched Hydee intently as he spoke.

'I shan't tell him what I've been doing while he's been away.' Hydee's words had an objective quality which produced a frown on Gasper's brow. She knew he was remembering that she was in love with her husband, and yet she had no incentive to guard herself against Carlos's displeasure.

'Very well, Hydee, my home it is.'

Chapter Eleven

A gentle breeze stirred the pine trees and chestnuts and the flag on the central tower of the Palacio as Hydee stood on the terrace listening to the children's laughter and recalling vividly the first time she had heard it. So much had been at stake then . . . and so much had happened since that it was hard to believe it was little more than two months since she had come to Portugal and to the Quinta de Manrique.

Two short months since she had been plain Miss Merrill, and now she was the Marquesa de Alva Manrique, wife of a Portuguese nobleman with whom she had made a marriage of convenience and with whom she had been foolish enough to fall in love.

In love with a man who, she knew, loved another woman, the beautiful Arminda, whose background was as noble and illustrious as that of the man she had hoped to win for a husband.

Hydee's thoughts returned to the children as she heard them laughing again, and then the laughter stopped and they were speaking in Portuguese. It was impossible for her to understand the conversation they were carrying on as they played and ran about, but she heard the word 'mama' and a smile touched her lips to give her face a glancing tenderness and enchanting beauty of which she was entirely unaware. She listened intently, hearing it again, this time from Ramos, who then said in English, 'I love her more than you do!'

'No you don't!'

Happiness lit her eyes despite the bitterness within her, and it was at that moment that she heard footsteps and swung around to look into the bronzed and handsome face of her husband. Her heart grew cold but her expression did not change to reveal her torment, and she heard Carlos say, 'You look particularly charming today, Hydee. What is it?'

'I was listening to the children,' she answered coolly. 'They were talking about me.'

'Yes, I heard them. They were arguing as to which one loves you the most.' He paused, but she had nothing to say. It was a silent moment, tense and with something unfathomable in the atmosphere.

'It was wonderful to hear it,' she said stiffly.

'Very gratifying,' he agreed. And then, 'You're obviously happy about the children and the way they've accepted you, but are you still happy about our relationship?'

Her eyes flew to his. 'I don't know what you

mean,' she quavered, wondering if he were about to
tell her he had made a mistake in marrying her. He'd
been home less than four hours, having arrived at
half-past eleven that morning, and when she inquired if his business had been conducted successfully, he merely said yes, offering nothing more. But
he had seemed preoccupied, and across the lunch-
eon table Hydee had caught him looking oddly at
her as if he had something on his mind which concerned her as much as himself. But he had gone to
his study afterwards and she had not seen him
again until now.

'I just wondered, that was all.'

'It's a strange thing to bring up, Carlos.' Her voice
was low and dignified; she seemed to be imbued with
an added pride, as if nature were providing her with
an armour against the feeling of inferiority she had
known from the very first, caused mainly, she supposed, by the attitude of her husband's family rather
than by Carlos himself. 'You must have a reason.
What is it?' Her words were a demand, and she saw
his eyes darken a little as if he resented her temerity.

'Never mind,' he returned abruptly. 'Forget it.'
And he strode away, going back to his study. The
next time Hydee saw him was at the dinner table. It
was an almost silent meal, and when it was over
Carlos said he was very tired and was going to bed.

Hydee forced herself to take a stroll in the garden,
choosing one of her favourite paths through delight-
ful masses of flowers—azaleas and roses, arum lilies
and camellias and many others, some blooming
together, others having been planted for the purpose
of having colour in the garden for most of the year.
Now, in the moonlight, only the perfumes were real.
Hydee inhaled over and over again, trying desper-

ately to divert her thoughts, seeking relief from the pressing agony of her situation.

As the moments passed, anger transcended all else, anger against the man who had brought something intimate and personal into a relationship which ought not to have been closer than that of nanny and employer. That was how it had begun and how Carlos had given her to understand it would continue. The fact that she had fallen in love with him had no bearing on the matter, because it was her own private affair, a circumstance unknown to Carlos, who had taken her for the pleasure of the moment without thought to what her feelings might be.

Her anger had abated somewhat by the time she was in her bedroom, yet as she stared at the closed door behind which her husband was probably sleeping soundly by now, she was assailed by a surge of indignation and humiliation which swiftly brought in its wake a resolve to keep him out of her room altogether. If he wanted physical satisfaction, then let him go back to Arminda!

She showered and slid between the cool white sheets, only to lie awake for several hours before falling into a short and fitful sleep. So she was not at her brightest when she went into the nursery to get the children ready for school the next morning. However, she did manage to hide her tiredness so that neither the children nor Carlos noticed anything unusual.

At the breakfast table they chatted as was customary, but Carlos seemed in no mood either to listen or to participate, and Hydee breathed a sigh of relief when eventually she was able to say, 'Come along, you two, it's time you were moving.'

'I wish it was a holiday,' sighed Ramos. 'How long is it to Christmas?'

'About seven weeks,' replied Hydee.

'That's a long time.'

'You'll be wearing bigger shoes by then,' laughed his sister, with a saucy glance in her father's direction, 'so you'll get more in the one you leave on the mantelpiece!'

'Shoe . . . ?' Hydee looked from one to the other, a bewildered expression on her face.

'In Portugal we put a shoe on the mantelpiece at Christmas and we have our presents put in it.'

'Some of our presents,' submitted Luisa. 'Only the little ones; the big ones are put in a bag and set on the hearth, aren't they, Papa?'

'Yes, that's right.' He was looking at his wife as he spoke. 'It's our custom to put our shoes out on Christmas Eve before we go to bed.'

'That sounds an unusual and charming idea.'

'It's unusual to you, Hydee, but not to us; it's what we've always been used to.'

Later, Hydee went out for her driving lesson, and on her return she saw Arminda's beautiful sleek limousine standing on the forecourt of the Palacio, and something froze within her. How dare the woman come here!

Fury born of jealousy led Hydee to the salon, where she suspected Arminda would be. But as she reached the half-open door, she heard her name mentioned and stopped abruptly. It was Arminda's mother, Dona Lucia, who was speaking, in English, much to Hydee's surprise.

'Arminda's heartbroken, Carlos—but you don't need me to tell you that. What is to come of this business? Why did you go to London, to be with her all that time, if you had no intention of doing something about this impetuous marriage of yours?'

'You know why I was with her in London.' Carlos paused, but the woman did not speak, and after a moment Carlos added, 'Arminda wouldn't have made a good and affectionate mother for my children. You must realise, Dona Lucia, that whatever my feelings are for Arminda, I must put my children's happiness first.'

'You say this about my daughter, implying that she's hard and wouldn't take to another woman's children, but you have no proof, Carlos! You merely make an assumption. Well, I haven't come here to spend time in that sort of argument or complaint; I have come to see what you intend to do about putting your mistake right. You'll not deny you love Arminda, I hope?'

An agonising pain struck at the nerves in Hydee's head as she began to walk away, slowly, because her legs seemed to be leaden weights beneath her.

'I can't deny it, can I? But I had to make the sacrifice in order to ensure my children's happiness, which, Dona Lucia, will always come before mine. . . .'

Going to the telephone, Hydee rang Gasper. 'I want to come out with you,' she said dully. 'Please come and fetch me.'

'What's wrong?' began Gasper, but Hydee interrupted him.

'Please come and fetch me,' she begged. 'I must get away.'

'All right,' he agreed. 'In about half an hour.'

'I'll meet you along the road, by the ruins of the old monastery.'

'I'll be there,' he promised, and the next moment there was silence on the line.

Hydee wrote a note for Carlos, which she gave to Caterina. The girl was in Hydee's room, returning some newly laundered dresses and blouses to her wardrobe, and Hydee sat down and penned the short note saying she was going out with Gasper and would not be in for lunch. Caterina looked at the name on the sealed envelope and then at her sad-eyed mistress.

'I will give it to him, Dona Hydee,' she said gently. 'You are going out?'

'That's right, Caterina. And as Dom Carlos is presently engaged, I can't disturb him, so that's the reason I am giving you the note.' Aware of the girl's intent gaze, Hydee turned away, going over to the wardrobe to pick out one of the pretty cotton dresses which Caterina had just hung there. Caterina was puzzled, mainly by the fact that Hydee had not given the note to Bento, who was the more obvious person to deliver it to his master. Caterina probably knew of Bento's attitude towards his new mistress; he was civil, and that was about all. He often spoke in Portuguese and had to be corrected by Carlos, as he had once been corrected by Gasper. Hydee thought he would have used his own language all the time had he dared.

'Will you be out when the children come from school?' inquired Caterina respectfully. 'If so, I will be sure to be here, even though today is one of my half-days off.'

A thoughtful pause followed as Hydee tried to think how long she wished to be away. 'I don't want to upset any plans you've made, Caterina,' she began.

'You won't be,' the girl was swift to assure her. 'You see, my Luiz is not off until tomorrow, so I'll be on my own anyway.'

'Luiz is off tomorrow, and you today? That's not very convenient for you, Caterina. Why didn't you ask me to change your free time to coincide with that of your fiancé?'

'I would never have asked so much,' returned Caterina, faintly horrified at the very idea.

Hydee smiled and said, 'I wouldn't have considered it presumptuous, Caterina, not at all. In the future you must have your free time when Luiz has his. Let me know about the changes just so I won't expect you to come at my call.' Hydee's voice was low and gracious, her smile friendly and sincere.

'That is most kind and considerate of you, senhora. Both Luiz and I will be happier to have our free time together.'

Hydee looked at the letter she had placed on the dressing table. 'Give it to my husband after his visitor has left,' she said.

'Yes, of course.' Caterina turned away as she spoke, and there was a strange huskiness in her voice as she added, 'Do you want me to take the children when they come from school, senhora?'

'I might be back, but if I'm not, then, yes, look to their tea, please, Caterina. And you'll have your half-day tomorrow instead of today.'

When the girl had left the room, Hydee changed quickly, brushed her hair and hurried from the Palacio via a stairway leading to a side door, then walked briskly along the drive to reach the main road just as Gasper was drawing his car onto the grass verge. She got in after a swift greeting and he drove off to find a place where he could turn the car around.

'What's happened?' he inquired when they were on their way to his home. 'I take it Carlos is back?'

'Yes; he returned yesterday afternoon.'

'And Isobella spilled the beans after all?' Hydee heard him grit his teeth and was quick to tell him that as yet Isobella had not contacted her brother.

'I don't think she will tell him about us,' she added. 'You frightened her with your threat of retaliation.' Hydee leant back against the soft leather upholstery and tried to relax.

'She knew I meant it. Eunice wasn't the only one who had things to hide—not that she managed to hide her indiscretions, but up till now Isobella has, probably because they're not so numerous. Isobella has one lover, whereas Eunice . . .' Gasper drew to the side of the narrow road as two cars, bumper to bumper, wanted to pass him. 'What's wrong, then, if it isn't Isobella?'

'Arminda's mother's there; she called while I was having my driving lesson. I . . . I heard a little of the conversation,' she went on, flushing slightly at the admission. 'It's true that Carlos was with Arminda in London, and it's also true that he's in love with her.' Hydee heard the angry indrawn breath taken by her companion and went on to relate all she had heard. 'So you can imagine that I wanted to get away for a while in order to think things out,' she added finally.

'And you wanted comfort and a sympathetic ear,' he observed.

'That's right. You promised to be my friend.'

'I shall remain your friend as long as you need me,' he said.

'You're very kind, Gasper.'

'Kind?' He slowed down to look at her profile, and she could not help but notice the tensed and grim set of his mouth and jaw, the nerve which throbbed in his cheek. 'It's not kindness, Hydee,' he said gently, 'it's love.'

Chapter Twelve

It was after five o'clock in the afternoon when Gasper drove up to the Palacio and dropped Hydee at the front door. 'You're sure you don't want me to come in with you?' he asked. 'I will, you know. Carlos doesn't frighten me.'

Hydee shook her head, smiling faintly at him. 'No, Gasper, I shall be all right. Carlos had better not say anything to me, because I'm not in the mood to be browbeaten.' It had been a strange few hours she had spent with Gasper; her first reaction after he had shocked her with the simple but dramatic declaration that he was in love with her, had been to ask him to turn around and take her back to the Palacio. But she had hesitated because she was so desperate-

141

ly unhappy that she had no wish to go home just yet. And, as if divining her thoughts, Gasper quickly assured her that she had nothing to worry about; he would not molest her or worry her in any way at all. He knew he had no chance, for not only was she married, but she was in love with her husband.

'I had to tell you,' he said as they sat on the shady plant-filled terrace eating a lunch of stuffed squid and green salad, 'because I believe perfect honesty is imperative in our relationship, Hydee. We have a lot in common, not the least of which is our intense and very excusable dislike for my family, which is also your husband's family. They will never accept you, and as for me, well, I am the cross they have to bear, the black sheep. Don't ever think I shall forget my place, Hydee. I consider it enough to be your gallant, your champion and protector in situations which could be ordeals for you, were you totally alone. You are not alone and never will be while I'm around.' He had looked straight at her with unquestionable sincerity. 'I want you to trust me, Hydee. Will you promise to do that always?'

She nodded, too full of emotion at first to articulate words, but eventually she heard herself say, 'Yes, Gasper, I promise.'

'And if ever you should want me, as you wanted me today, don't hesitate to let me know.'

'I won't.' Again she had been emotionally affected to the point where speech was difficult. She had a true and trustworthy friend in Gasper, flirt and philanderer though he was with other women, and she meant to hold on to that friendship no matter what objections Carlos might make, or what criticism she might encounter from the rest of his family.

She went slowly up the wide steps to the front

door. It was locked, and as she had not brought her key with her, she had to use the ornate silver-gilt knocker. Bento came, his mouth a straight unsmiling line in his round masklike countenance, his critical eyes covertly examing her face.

'Dom Carlos told me to say that he wishes to see you as soon as you come in, senhora,' he said in an expressionless tone of voice. 'He is in his study now.'

'Thank you.' She walked stiffly past him with head held high. Outwardly she was calm enough, but, as always when she was in any way disturbed, her stomach muscles were tying themselves into hard little knots.

She tapped softly, heard a curt 'Come in' and entered, closing the door quietly behind her. Their eyes met across the room, Carlos's glacier cold with anger, hers defiant but unnaturally bright for all that. He was standing with his back to the window, a towering, formidable figure, dark of countenance and arrogant of bearing. In the end it was Hydee who broke the silence.

'You want to see me, Carlos? Bento gave me the message.'

'The note you left . . .' He thumbed towards the desk on which it lay, one edge fluttering, caught in the breeze from an overhead fan. 'What exactly does it mean?'

Hydee swallowed convulsively but her voice was steady and clear as she replied, a question in her gaze, 'I should have thought it was plain enough, Carlos. Is something puzzling you?'

His dark eyes glittered dangerously. She had seen him angry before, but never in such a temper as this; there was no doubt about his being furious now.

'I advise you not to adopt that attitude with me,'

143

he said. 'I demand to know why you went off for the day with Gasper.'

'Demand?' she repeated, playing for time and wondering why she had not rehearsed what she would say in answer to the questions he must inevitably ask. 'I don't care for that word, Carlos.'

'Stop procrastinating,' he thundered, taking a step towards her. 'What was your reason for going out with Gasper—and staying out all day? Answer me at once!'

The colour was slowly receding from her face because, despite what she had said to Gasper, she was afraid of her husband, and as fear always bred anger with Hydee, she shot out an answer which she immediately felt she might come to regret. 'I went out with him because I overheard part of a conversation between you and Dona Lucia! I already knew you'd been with Arminda in London, and then this came on top! What did you expect me to do—stay here and fawn on you or something? I went where I was wanted—*wanted,* do you hear!'

'I should imagine the entire household can hear,' he answered, but he, too, was pale now—no, it was a ghastly grey that discoloured the gleaming tan of his face, and his eyes seemed almost stricken, deepening in their sockets.

But it did not take long for his innate self-command to come to the fore, and when next he spoke, it was in a smooth urbane voice that effectively covered his previous discomposure. 'So you overheard my conversation with Dona Lucia? Am I to take it that you deliberately listened at the door?' Contempt was in his voice, but Hydee was shrewd enough to know that he was still a good deal put out by her revelation.

'It was partly an accident, partly deliberate. You must remember that I already knew Arminda was with you in London. When I saw her car, I wanted to walk in on the two of you. . . .' Hydee's voice was defiant, challenging, her big eyes bright with anger and unshed tears. 'I heard my name mentioned and naturally wanted to know what that woman was saying about me!'

For a moment he remained silent, and then, on an indrawn breath that was something between a sigh and an expression of anger, he said, 'It's a pity we weren't speaking in Portuguese.'

'A great pity! However, you weren't, and so I heard you admit to being in love with Arminda.'

He seemed to flinch, but when he spoke it was to ask, 'Who told you I was with Arminda in London?'

'I'm not willing to say.'

'It must have been Gasper; there isn't much that goes on in our family that escapes his notice.'

'It wasn't Gasper—at least, he only verified what I'd already been told.'

'Then someone else knew?' He was plainly disturbed, and Hydee, in her present state of anger and with the desire to hit back, flashed at him with contempt, 'I expect a great many people knew. A man in your position can't carry on an affair without it giving rise to scandal.' Carlos said nothing, but into the greyness of his face there crept a hint of crimson, evidence that he'd received a blow where it could hurt him most. He was a nobleman, highly respected, almost revered by his estate workers, and the thought of his name being bandied about must be an intolerable sting to his pride.

'Who was it who told you about my being with Arminda in London?' he asked again.

Hydee paused, fully aware that if she said it was his sister then he would tackle her at once. Isobella's response would be to reveal what she had seen between Hydee and Gasper, for in her fury she would probably forget all about Gasper's threatened reprisal.

After a prolonged moment of indecision Hydee felt she had little to lose. It was time Carlos knew exactly what kind of mischief-maker Isobella was. 'Your sister told me,' she informed him tautly. 'She called specifically to let me know that Arminda was in London.'

Carlos stared, and it seemed an eternity before he spoke. 'Isobella did a thing like that?'

'I've already told you she doesn't like me, and you know why she doesn't. It was her wish that you would marry her friend Arminda, whom you love—and I can't see why you didn't marry her, because you could have engaged a nanny for the children—'

'You already know that a nanny wasn't the answer. My children needed something more; they needed a mother—'

'And so you chose me!' she cut in wrathfully. 'You used me for your own unscrupulous ends! But if you'd no intention of giving Arminda up, why did you make love to me?' Her eyes blazed; she waited for a reply, and when none came, she repeated her question. 'You can't answer,' she added at once, her mouth curling with contempt, 'because you don't want to admit it was merely for convenience!' As her eyes covered the length of his body in a roving glance of contempt, she saw his mouth compress, his hands clench at his sides. He was in a white-hot fury, but nothing could deter her now. 'You're the most despicable man I've ever known! To have a mistress—

Oh, yes, that is in fact a *delicate* name for her, so you needn't look at me like that! To have a mistress and yet make love to me was the act of a man totally without scruples, because you weren't even being faithful to the woman you loved! You took me out of selfishness, for convenience—because Arminda wasn't at hand. That was the reason, wasn't it?'

He met her gaze, black fury in his eyes. Hydee's heart was already beating overtime, but now every nerve in her body rioted, for it almost seemed that he would do her physical injury. The very air was filled with the ghastly fury of them both, the deep silence broken only by the heavy ticking of the clock on the wall. Carlos's lips moved convulsively; a nerve pulsated violently in his throat. Hydee had the impression that although gripped in the throes of an anger of violent proportions, he was fighting desperately to control the words that hovered on his lips. But as Hydee's eyes again swept him with utter contempt in their depths, Carlos seemed to lose control and the words he uttered were the cruellest Hydee would ever hear in the whole of her life.

'I made love to you because you wanted it, *asked* for it! You said you regretted marrying me, that there was nothing in your life—that you needed something more. Well, I'd have been totally obtuse if I hadn't known what the "something more" was, *so I gave it to you!*'

Silence, as Hydee swayed unsteadily on her feet, her face deathly white, her beautiful eyes dilating as inexpressible horror and shame looked out from their depths.

'So that was why you . . . you m-made love t-to me?' Words came at last, voiced in accents husky and broken by the pain and disillusionment his heartless statement had inflicted on her. 'At the time I believed it meant something to you, if only that you were deriving pleasure. . . .' She stopped, staring at him through stricken eyes before burying her head in her hands. 'Oh, no,' she cried in a muffled voice. 'What must you have thought of me? Assuming that I was craving . . . physical satisfaction.' She withdrew her hands but turned away, unable to look at him, not caring if she never saw his face again. But she managed to say over her shoulder, as she moved to the door on legs that felt almost too weak to support her, 'You might not believe me when I say that after I learned about your being with Arminda in London, I'd resolved never to sleep with you again.' At the door she stopped but did not turn her head. 'That happens to be how much I craved physical satisfaction. Were I the woman you took me for, I'd not care if you had a dozen mistresses so long as you spared *me* a little of your time!'

'Hydee!' Her name rang out across the room as she opened the door. 'How dare you talk to me like that?'

She did turn then. 'I trust you will get another nanny for your children as soon as possible—'

'Nanny?'

She looked directly into his eyes. 'That is what I am, Carlos, nothing more. Get someone else immediately or arrange for Caterina to take care of them. I shall be leaving just as soon as it can be arranged.'

'Hydee!' he called again, but she paid no heed as she closed the door softly behind her, conscious of Bento moving just as silently as he made his way to the far end of the hall where the servants' quarters were situated.

Chapter Thirteen

A nameless dread lay heavy across Hydee's heart as she went out into the grounds of the Palacio, craving the peace and isolation which the remote paths provided. She had burned her bridges, had stated quite emphatically her desire to leave her husband. He could not prevent her, nor, she supposed, would he try. Yet what was she to do now?

Ellie's last letter had contained the information that she had given the owner of the flat notice that she was leaving, and already he had tenants ready to move in as soon as Ellie moved out. So Hydee had neither a home nor a job to go back to when she returned to England. And as she wandered aimlessly along the flower-bordered paths, she blamed herself entirely for what was happening to her. After what Noel had done, she had sworn never to marry, and yet she had so easily been persuaded, even in the face of Ellie's repeated warnings.

What must she do? she asked herself again. She had a little money saved from the generous allowance Carlos had given her, but that wouldn't last long. Tears filled her eyes, tears of regret and self-pity, but those that came afterwards were hot and bitter, shed because of her love for Carlos, which she felt would never fade even though he had treated her even more callously than Noel had. Carlos had used her and scorned her, considering her beneath him; he had tried to deny her the friendship of the only member of his family who treated her in any way as an equal. The others had not even afforded her the measure of respect which good breeding demanded.

Gasper. . . .

It was natural that his name and image should remain in her mind, but as yet she could not bring herself to enlist his help. She had to think of the children, who had come to love her, to depend on her, to expect her to be there every morning to get them ready for school, to meet them on their return and take tea with them, after which they would play on the lawn or she would read to them as they all sat close in one of the numerous little arbors in the grounds of the Palacio. It was she who bathed them and put them to bed each evening, who kissed them good night.

It would be tantamount to cruelty just to walk out on them, she thought, but the thought served only to increase her misery because she wanted nothing more at this time than to shake the dust of the Palacio off her heels immediately.

Suddenly she felt the hairs on her forearms tingle and rise as a shadow was thrown across the path from behind. She turned, stepping to one side to allow Carlos to pass, then felt foolish because it was plain that he was here because he had been looking for her and wanted to talk.

He stopped just in front of her, preventing any further progress. She looked up into the impenetrable mask of a face, cold and grey, the eyes hard, the mouth a thin tight line—ruthless, she thought—and his voice was icily remote as he said, 'I'm glad I found you, Hydee.' He gave her a speculative, measuring look. 'I wondered if you'd gone running to Gasper.'

'I intend to phone him later.' Her own voice was cold, her eyes defiant in case he should try to forbid her to follow her own inclinations. 'I shall ask him to take me to his home, so I shan't be in for dinner this evening.' To her surprise Carlos allowed that to pass without comment.

'Why aren't you with the children?'

Looking into his face, she knew instinctively that the question was automatic and not what he had at first intended to say. He seemed unsure of himself, faintly humble in spite of his innate arrogance.

'Caterina is looking after them today. She offered and I accepted because I had no idea what time I would be back.' There was dignity in her tone and bearing. Carlos stared at her and seemed to swallow something hard and unpleasant in his throat.

'I would like to talk to you, Hydee. Will you come into the house?'

She shook her head. There was nothing she

151

wanted to discuss with him, not now that the sweetness of her love was dissolved in pain, her rosy dreams shattered, leaving nothing but fragments impossible to restore.

'I have no wish to talk to you,' she returned quietly.

'I want to ask you to stay—'

'I can't . . .' she began, but her voice trailed away to silence.

'You care for the children and they care for you, Hydee. You can't abandon them in cold blood like this.'

Was he pleading—or merely playing on her obvious weakness for Ramos and Luisa?

'I asked you to find someone else,' was Hydee's pointed reminder.

'Yes, but I gained the impression that you wanted to leave almost immediately.'

'I shall have to think about it,' she answered after a moment of consideration.

'Then you're not leaving at once?'

'I've just said I'll have to think about it.'

Carlos frowned. 'I feel sure you won't go yet awhile—'

'What makes you so sure?' demanded Hydee, marvelling at her own temerity, at the self-confidence she was affecting, standing up to him, in fact, just as if she were his equal.

'Your nature,' he began when she interrupted him.

'You know nothing of my nature! Otherwise you'd never have jumped to the conclusion you did regarding . . .' She trailed off, colouring delicately, appearing very young and lovely in her rush of embarrassment.

'I admit to making a mistake about that, and I apologise—'

'But not humbly!' she flashed. 'Don't lower your pride, Carlos! Keep in mind your most exalted position—and keep your apology! I don't want it!'

'I do understand how you feel,' he owned.

'Then let us leave it at that!' Brushing past him, she hurried on, frowning as she heard his steps behind her. 'Go away! Go and find Arminda if you're short of someone to talk to.'

'I must know your plans, Hydee,' he insisted.

'I have no immediate plans.' She was almost in tears, but it was not her intention to let him see them fall. 'I've had no time to think, but I shall let you know what I've decided just as soon as my mind is made up.'

'If you would stay until after Christmas,' he began, 'I'd be grateful.'

'Grateful?' Hydee swung around, her eyes examining his face. 'How much did it cost you to use a word like that, I wonder?' No answer, just a fleeting scowl and then nothing but an unreadable mask. 'I don't think I want to stay that long.' She thought of the children again, and she thought of Ellie and Ray, who had planned to have their honeymoon here. 'I . . . I . . .' She swallowed convulsively but still contrived to hold back her tears. 'I've said I'll let you know—please leave it at that.'

'Very well,' he agreed after a small hesitation. And then, his tones ringing harsh and cold, 'Were you serious about not being at home for dinner this evening?'

'If Gasper is in, I shall dine at his home.'

Carlos gritted his teeth, opened his mouth to say something and then closed it again, much to Hydee's satisfaction. At last, it seemed, he lacked the confidence to assert his authority and forbid her to go out. He was afraid of upsetting her, now that he wanted something important from her.

He strode away without another word. Only then did Hydee let the scalding tears fall onto her cheeks.

Gasper came for her at half-past seven. She had said little on the phone, and Gasper had not wasted time on questions which could be asked later.

Although Carlos was at the window of one of the downstairs rooms, he made no attempt to stop Hydee from getting into the car. The first thing she said as they drove away was, 'I'm causing a rift between you and Carlos, aren't I?'

'We've never been close.' Gasper's voice was terse and grim. He asked her what had happened to make her decide to come out like this.

She related everything, watching his profile, its changing shape as his jaw went taut and his mouth compressed. 'So it's come to a head. He admitted he's in love with Arminda?'

'He didn't deny it, which is in effect an admission.'

Gasper had to agree. 'So what are your plans, Hydee?' he asked, turning when he saw her handkerchief appear.

'Carlos wants me to stay until after Christmas, but I haven't made up my mind. I do feel awful about leaving the children, and also there's Ellie.' She had already told him that Ellie was coming over for her honeymoon. 'On the other hand, Gasper, how can I stay after what's happened?'

Gasper became thoughtful for a time and then said, 'In making up your mind, don't disregard the fact that there are many people in our family who would be delighted to see you go, Hydee. Have you thought of the satisfaction your departure would give Isobella alone?' There was a note of grimness in the reminder.

'She said the marriage wouldn't last six months,' reflected Hydee, a sob in her voice.

'Personally, I'd never hand her a triumph like that. However, it's your decision.' Gasper's voice was low, controlled, but Hydee sensed his deep concern for her, and his own unhappiness.

'You think I ought to stay?'

'If you can bear to, yes, I do. Why should you leave your home?' He became quiet while negotiating several tight bends in the road. 'What would you do if you went back to England?'

'That's the problem, Gasper,' she admitted, going on to tell him that she would have neither home nor job to go to.

'In that case,' he said, 'my advice is to stay.'

'You seem to forget that I'm in love with Carlos,' she said simply, and heard the little indrawn breath whose meaning she was unable to define. 'It would be unbearable to stay indefinitely.'

'Yes,' he agreed, 'I expect it would.'

'Besides, the sooner I'm away from him, the sooner I shall begin to forget.' Inevitably she remembered Noel, and the heartache when he had jilted her. But at least she had Ellie living with her, whereas this time she would have no one.

'It's as bad as that?'

She nodded, a surge of desolation sweeping over her that was almost physical, so acute was the pain. She could not speak, and as Gasper also seemed disinclined to talk, the rest of the drive continued in silence.

As Gasper had told his chef he would be bringing a guest back with him, the table was laid for two. The menu was freshly roasted *cabrito* with rice and spinach. Vine-ripened strawberries with cream came as dessert, and all was washed down with the young green wine, *vinho verde*.

'You've eaten well, under the circumstances,' Gasper observed later with satisfaction. They were on the patio with their coffee, enjoying the cool fresh breeze as they sat beneath the trellised vines in the pale amber glow of the lights subtly hidden in the foliage above their heads.

It was after midnight when at last Gasper took Hydee home, and she was no sooner in her bedroom than the communicating door swung open and Carlos, fully dressed and looking somewhat haggard, demanded to know what had made her so late. He was angry, a vein standing out in his temple, but he preserved a calm exterior.

'That,' she answered, casting him a scornful glance, 'is my business. I don't even know what time you used to leave Arminda—if you left her at all.'

He let that pass, much to her surprise. 'I won't have you staying out till midnight with my cousin,' he told her harshly. 'The servants will know what time you came in, and there'll be gossip!'

'Bento knows what time I came in, but it so happens that I don't care a rap for his opinion.'

'Have you no thought for me?' Carlos spoke more soberly, his features tensed, his lids heavy as though he were overtired.

'Did you have any thought for me when you stayed in London with Arminda?' she countered.

'I didn't stay with Arminda in the way you be-

156

lieve,' he said. 'However, there's nothing to be gained by my trying to vindicate myself, because I do care deeply for Arminda—' He stopped abruptly as Hydee flinched, and he turned from her then to go into his own room. Hydee heard the door click, very softly, as if he did not want her to hear and yet at the same time was desirous of putting a fully closed door between them.

Hydee stood for a long while staring at the door, thinking of what he had said about not staying with Arminda in the way she had believed. His words were tantamount to a denial of any intimacy between them. Could that be true? Isobella had said they were lovers, but Hydee would rather take Carlos's word, even now, than that of his sister. However, the vital and wounding words had come afterwards: 'I do care deeply for Arminda. . . .'

Hydee continued to stare at the door, wondering how long she would be able to remain here, loving her husband as she did, and yet having to endure, every night, the sight of that closed door. At Christmas she would also have to endure seeing him with Arminda, with Isobella there watching, that sneering mouth curved in triumph, those dark eyes scorching in their contempt. She thought about the other relatives who would be staying at the Palacio for Christmas, and the ordeal she would be forced to undergo. No, it was unthinkable that she should stay, but after a night's rest, which was surprisingly undisturbed, Hydee felt differently; she felt she could stay until after the holiday, if only for the children's sake.

After breakfast she rang Gasper to tell him of her decision.

'Only till after Christmas?' he said, and the note of disappointment in his voice was not difficult to detect. 'Why not indefinitely?'

'It would be impossible,' she replied.

'So until Christmas it is, then?'

'Yes.' A small pause ensued. 'I know the party might be an ordeal, with the whole family staying here, but I shall have you for an ally, and my two friends, Ellie and Ray, as an added support.'

'Four against the whole bunch.' Gasper gave a low laugh. 'The odds are very much in favour of the patricians, but I daresay the plebs will manage to keep them at bay!'

Hydee found herself catching his mood, and surprised herself when she laughed.

'Good girl,' Gasper applauded. 'Keep that chin of yours up, whatever happens. Promise me?'

'Yes, Gasper,' she answered softly. 'I promise.' And as she put the receiver on its rest, she thought how ironic it was that she should have fallen in love twice with men who did not want her, and now that Gasper had fallen in love with her, *she* did not want *him*—not in that way, at least. In any case, much as she liked him and valued his friendship, Hydee was under no illusions as to his basic character. He lacked the makings of a faithful husband as well as the vital attraction Carlos possessed to such a great degree.

Chapter Fourteen

As the days drifted slowly by, Hydee began to realise she had been steered into a path she had not really wanted to take. The wisest course would have been to go away immediately, remove herself from the Palacio and its unhappy memories. She had been influenced first by her concern for others—the children and their happiness at Christmas, and Ellie's honeymoon. Second, she had heeded the advice proffered by Gasper, who obviously hated the idea of Isobella's triumph if Hydee should leave her husband. Third, there had been the floundering disorder of her own mind when she tried to formulate plans for her future. The difficulty of finding a home and then a job, of resettling her life into some sort of routine and pattern, had all seemed too much for her. Those difficulties must be tackled sometime, there was no doubt about that, but for the present she would stay on at the Palacio, despite the hardship that entailed for herself.

She had seen little of her husband, who had gone to Lisbon on business and decided to stay there for several days. Isobella had called before he went, and the haste with which she departed had left Hydee in no doubt that her brother had admonished her for what she had done. In turn Isobella retaliated in the way Hydee had expected her to; but when approached by Carlos, Hydee had been more than ready with her answer.

'And if we were kissing each other, what of it? At least we weren't sleeping together!'

His teeth had snapped together and his dark eyes had smouldered like embers newly fanned. 'Nor did Arminda and I sleep together. I've already told you, I didn't stay with Arminda in the way you believe.'

Hydee let that pass, but it had remained with her, as it had when he first said it. Although she found herself believing him, accepting that he and Arminda were not lovers, at the same time she was agonisingly conscious of the admission he had made about caring deeply for the girl.

Hydee was in the nursery when Luisa and Ramos bounded in from school, full of life, eyes taking on an added glow as they saw Hydee there, busying herself with simple tasks, the one on which she was presently occupied being the tidying up of Ramos's bookshelves.

'Oh. . . . Is there anything to eat, Mama?' Luisa stood before her, looking up, a dovelike expression in her eyes. 'I like you being here when we come in,' she said. 'Sometimes you aren't here, and it's . . . it's funny.'

'She means strange,' elucidated her brother knowledgeably. 'The nursery seems like it is when we've been away on holiday and we come back—empty and sort of . . . cold.' Ramos looked at Hydee and added, 'Do you know what I mean?'

She nodded her head. 'Yes, Ramos, I do know what you mean. I must try always to be here when you come in, mustn't I?'

'Papa said you have to go out sometimes.'

'He did? When?'

'I can't remember. But I talked to him about it when you weren't in one day. Caterina came soon and said she was making our tea and having it with us instead of you.'

'You like Caterina, though?'

'Yes. She's nice, but we want you, Mama—always! Don't we, Luisa?'

For answer the child hugged Hydee's knees, rubbing her face against her skirt. 'Mama will be here always,' she stated. 'She's come to stay forever. Papa told us that when he and Mama got married.'

'Yes, I remember.'

With a sigh Hydee put the child from her and rang for the tea to be brought up. When it was eaten, they went out to the garden and played ball on the lawn in front of the house. Hydee saw Gasper's car bowling along the drive and after a moment left the children to play on their own.

'Hello,' he greeted her as he examined her face, subjecting it to an intent scrutiny. 'How are things? I wanted to get over yesterday, but we had problems. My estate manager has taken ill and is in hospital in Lisbon. He might have to have an operation.'

'Oh, I'm sorry.' Hydee had met Henrique and liked him enormously. He had always treated her with the greatest respect, and never had she seen any of those covert glances which Bento so often sent in her direction. 'Will it be a serious operation?'

'Could be. However, let us hope for the best.' He was standing by his car, tall and distinguished, clad in casual slacks of fine white linen and a forest-green shirt open at the neck. 'Shall we go inside, or are you fully occupied with the children?' His eyes slid over to them, his hand lifting. They waved back, but there was no eagerness to run to him. Hydee felt sad at the lack of affection between the children and the man they called uncle, and knew it was owing to their father's disinterest in his cousin. Hydee found herself hoping that as they grew older, the children would come to see the good qualities in Gasper and not take the attitude of the rest of the family, joining them in lining up against him. Not that he was in any way troubled by the opinion of his family. Gasper took it all in stride, and his attitude was one of indifference not unmingled with disdain and a certain measure of pity. They were so self-centred, living in their own narrow but exalted world, concerned with no one but themselves and their circle of high-bred friends.

'I can leave them,' she decided. 'They had their tea a few minutes ago.'

'When do you expect Carlos back?' Gasper inquired a few minutes later as they sat on a large gold velvet couch flanking the massive fireplace, drinking sherry.

'I've no idea. We don't communicate much these days,' she added, and the sad inflection in her voice could not possibly escape him. He sighed exasperatedly.

'He's a fool if ever there was one! Arminda's beautiful, but that's about all she has to offer any man. She's hard and mercenary, with a love of herself stemming from pride in her beauty and her station. She has no real concern for anyone else, and what she wants from Carlos is nothing more than the status of being a marquesa.'

'He might be a fool, as you say, Gasper, but he happens to love her. And love is the most important thing. He can't help himself any more than I can help myself.'

'You still love him, in spite of everything?'

'I shall love him until I die,' she whispered. 'What I feel for him is something very different from what I felt for Noel.' She had confided in Gasper about Noel right at the beginning; he had said she was better without him, and she now admitted that Gasper had been right.

He stayed for dinner, and although profoundly aware of Bento's disapproval, Hydee ignored the man except when it was necessary to give him an order.

'I'd have that fellow out of here if I were Carlos!' snapped Gasper when Bento had spoken to him in Portuguese and been admonished for it. 'He's insolent!'

'I'm not worried about Bento,' Hydee assured him in a soothing tone. 'I shan't be here much longer. I've told Carlos I shall definitely be leaving immediately after Christmas, so if he doesn't replace me as nanny for Luisa and Ramos then, Caterina will have to look after them.'

'I hope we shan't lose touch?'

'There's no reason why we should,' she said, managing to produce a smile. She was watching Felix drawing the cork from a bottle of wine with an expertise which revealed regular practice. 'Perhaps you will take a holiday in England and we can meet.'

'Undoubtedly I shall meet you in England,' he declared. And then, lifting his glass after it had been filled, 'Here's to Christmas, and we'll not think beyond that for the present.'

Carlos arrived home the following day. Hydee happened to be on the balcony of her bedroom as he slid from his car and glanced up, catching sight of her even though she instinctively drew back, hoping the stone balustrade would hide her from his view.

Within five minutes he was in her bedroom, stepping through the window onto the balcony. She could only stare in surprise, twisting her neck in order to look at him. His eyes studied her intently for a moment before he spoke.

'Hydee, I'm going to ask you to stay here indefinitely.' Moving to one side, he reached for the vacant chair, turned it to face her, and then sat down. 'I've been thinking seriously about our situation. I never meant it to end like this—'

'You must surely have known it would end like this if you had no intention of giving Arminda up,' she cut in sharply. 'Besides, do you suppose *I* ever imagined it would be like this?' The pain of loving him and yet quarrelling this way was that of a dagger thrusting deep into her heart, but she felt she must resist any persuasion he might attempt to make. Getting away was becoming an obsession which made Christmas seem farther away than ever, causing the days to pass slowly, the nights in fitful tossing and turning. She spent the long hours counting the days off in the mental calendar of her mind.

'If you go back, you have no one, Hydee,' he persisted patiently. 'I'll give you money, of course—'

'I don't want your money!' she flashed at him, insulted by the offer. 'As for my having no one—why should you care? We'll get a divorce, and that will be the end of it.'

'Here in my country we don't speak so lightly of divorce as you are doing,' he chided.

'It's the only answer when two people don't get along. Doreen had a divorce, and she's a lot happier for it.'

Carlos frowned impatiently and made no comment; it would have been irrelevant anyway, Hydee now admitted as she waited for her husband to speak again.

'You'd have come as a nanny, remember?' She merely nodded, too emotionally upset to answer because she was thinking of her optimism when, after the first shock of being asked to be a mother and not a nanny, she had looked forward to a happy future. How little she knew at that time! How deeply she regretted not having taken her friend's advice. 'Well,' Carlos continued, 'I am asking you to *be* a nanny, to stay with the children at least until they no longer need you.'

Instinctively she shook her head, recalling her initial conviction that he would not try to keep her. 'I can't stay indefinitely. I'll stay until Christmas is over, and then I'm leaving you, Carlos.' Her tone was sad because she could not altogether hide her feelings, suppress her emotions, nor even control her expression. Carlos stared, a grimness playing about his mouth, his eyes dark, unfathomable. That he was emotionally affected was evident, and Hydee felt the stinging barb of jealousy pierce her heart because his thoughts must be with Arminda.

'Christmas isn't very far away,' Carlos reminded her. 'It won't be long.'

'Long enough for you to find a replacement for me.'

'One does not find a replacement for one's wife.' Soft the tone now, and almost gentle, but the change only served to anger her.

'Don't!' she flashed. 'Keep your gentle tone for the woman you love.'

He seemed unable to find anything to say, and in the uneasy silence Hydee rose from her chair and stood with her palms resting on the heavy stone railing, her gaze on the crystal spray of the fountain, glistening like a cascade of pure white diamonds in the light of a moon that was almost full. The air around her trembled; even at this time of year perfumes floated on the breeze. The grounds were chequered with shapes and patterns and colours— jade and emerald, smoke-grey and dun where shadows veiled the moonglow. Misty clouds pressed down on the valley sides, presaging a cool, dewy aspect when the light of a new day crept into the valley.

Hydee shivered and turned, saying quietly, 'I'm going in, Carlos. It's late.'

He did not move, and she left him sitting there, hoping he would not stay long, although he need not disturb her, since he could go into his own room via the balcony. To her surprise, he was in her room less than two minutes after she entered it herself. Frowning, she snapped, 'What do you want, Carlos?'

No answer, and suddenly his expression changed and he shortened the distance between them. Hydee stepped back, the colour receding from her face.

'Don't speak to me like that, Hydee,' he almost snarled. 'You're my wife!'

'In name only!'

'You could be expecting my child.'

'Your child?' He had mentioned it before, but now the situation had changed. 'Is that what you want?' She shook her head instantly, denying her own question. 'No, you'd never want my child, but it would keep me here, or so you believe. Well, let me disillusion you. I'd not stay even if I were having a child!' Nor would she let him know, she thought, praying with everything in her heart that she had escaped an eventuality such as that.

He moved again, and she took another step back, bringing her legs into contact with the huge four-poster bed. 'Go away,' she ordered, eyes flashing. 'I told you I didn't want you in my room again!' A mistake—perhaps not in the actual meaning of her words but in the way they were phrased, and also in the way they were delivered. Carlos's eyes smouldered, narrowing to dark, menacing slits.

'You're my wife!' he gritted. 'If I want to come to your room, then I shall come anytime I like.'

Hydee's disbelieving eyes were drawn to the slender brown hands coming up from his sides. She needed no extraordinary perception to guess what he had in mind. And yet part of her brain refused to accept the obvious, because for him to take her now would not only mean a lowering of his pride but also increase the contempt she already felt for him.

'I'm your wife in name only,' she repeated. 'I've just reminded you of it.' White to the lips now, she watched with fascinated eyes as his hands came forwards. But despite her position, which was one of near-imprisonment, for he was threateningly close, Hydee was galvanised into action, and even as his hands came out to grasp her arms, she pivoted on her heels, almost knocking him off balance by the urgency and violence of her manoeuvre. She sped to the door, but even as she reached it she felt his steely fingers close round her wrist and she came up against his muscular frame with an impact that left her panting and dazed. She stood staring up at him, tall and overpowering, masterfully arrogant, his body dominatingly flexed. A nobleman whose innate superiority was sustained even though his basic male instincts were swiftly reverting to the primitive.

'Let go of me!' she cried, twisting her wrist in a furious endeavour to free herself and gaining nothing but bruises. Tears rushed to her eyes, stiffening her lashes, but Carlos was in no mood for pity, or even for noticing her distress. All that penetrated his consciousness were her anger and rejection of him. Ruthlessly he took both her arms, brought her against his granite-hard body and possessed her lips, covering them moistly in a fierce and sensuous kiss that temporarily robbed her of breath. She placed her palms against the iron hardness of his chest, employing her puny strength as she attempted to increase the tiny space she had managed to put between his body and her own.

He soon had her two small hands in his grasp, imprisoned behind her back, while his other hand slid with arrogant possessiveness down the length of her spine to bring her body to his, melding her pliancy against his hardness with the deliberate intention of forcing her to accept that there was no escape from him, that total compliance was his demand and his intention.

She stopped struggling and resigned herself to his mastery, to the determined caress of his hand kneading her quivering flesh as it gradually ignited her desire for him, crushing the last vestige of resistance. Desire licked at her senses, and when she lifted her eyes to the arrogant mask of his, she swayed in surrender, offering her glowing lips, then parting them obediently in response to the fierce pressure inflicted on them. She was aware that his hand was at her back, felt the tautness of her dress slacken as the zip was released.

The dress soon lay at her feet, and she stared down at it, lips tingling with the pleasure-pain of his kisses, cheeks coloured by embarrassment. Suddenly there was only her love, and she lifted her head to examine his chiselled male features in a sort of desperate search for any small sign that it was not solely lust that was driving him to assert his rights. But all she encountered in those dark foreign eyes was desire; they were smouldering fuses ready to ignite, and even as she stared she saw them blaze, heard a guttural sound in the depths of his throat, and before she knew it, she was being crushed to his body again, her slender frame hurt by his strength, her breasts hard against his chest.

He bent his head, taking her lips fiercely, savagely, before, in staggering contrast, his mouth began to make a gentle exploration of her face, caressing her cheeks, her temples, and down again to the tender curve of her throat, his eyes dark with a profound tenderness. His hands, too, were tender and gentle, quickening her own need to pulsating life so that he did not really need to curl his long lean fingers round her soft flesh in order to arch her body against his.

Minutes later he was with her on the bed, his restless hands gliding over her warm flesh, caressing her sensitive places, while his lips hovered against her breasts, light and teasing, fanning her desire to the fierce flame of urgent, all-consuming need.

'Carlos . . . love me,' she whispered, but almost silently. He only saw her lips move, felt the current of yearning that swept through her lovely naked body, lying there beside him, in response to the questing freedom of his hands.

'Hydee. . . .' the word was uttered in a throaty bass tone, his lips against her cheek. The next moment their bodies were fused, the battering urgency of their mutual need swiftly transporting them to rapturous heights where all their earthly problems dissolved to insignificance.

Chapter Fifteen

On the day before the expected arrival of the honeymoon couple, Hydee sought her husband out in his study to ask if he would be willing to pretend that everything was all right between them.

'It would spoil their honeymoon if Ellie thought I was unhappy,' Hydee added unnecessarily. 'If . . . if you won't find it too difficult . . .' She let her voice trail off as her mind drifted away from the present to that memorable night when he had come to her in anger and in the end made love to her so gently. Although he had not come to her since, his whole manner had undergone a change from that night onwards. He was more friendly and communicative, seeming to derive pleasure from her company; he smiled more often, took a keen interest in what she wore and how she looked generally, making remarks which, though appearing to be guarded, could only be described as flattering. He was more tolerant regarding her friendship with Gasper, although on a couple of occasions when she had come in very late she had witnessed something akin to anger in her husband's attitude. On both occasions he had waited up for her, admonishing her for staying out so late. But Hydee had the impression that he was more pained than angry, and she supposed it was his pride that was being stung.

'I assure you I shall not find it difficult to act as if I am a happily married man.' Carlos's foreign voice was low, tinged with an inflection which was impossible to define.

Hydee coloured at his words and forced a thin smile to her lips. 'There isn't any need for that, Carlos. Ellie knows the details regarding our marriage.'

'She does?'

'Of course. She shared my flat so she knew I'd applied for the post of nanny. . . .' Hydee broke off, shrugging. 'She knows it all,' she ended briefly.

'I see. So she won't expect either of us to be demonstrative?'

'No.' Hydee had to smile, for she could not for the life of her imagine Carlos being demonstrative in public.

'What makes you smile?' he wanted to know.

She told him, and he looked at her with a curious expression. However, all he said was, 'You can rely on me not to do or say anything that will upset your friend.'

'Thank you, Carlos. I'm grateful to you.'

He frowned, but made no comment, changing the subject easily as he asked if she was going to help decorate the Christmas tree. Her eyes lit up and her smile deepened to impart an added beauty to her face. 'You look so different when you're happy,' he observed, and again there was something unfathomable in his voice.

'I suppose most people look better when they're happy,' she said, averting her eyes lest she betray what was in her heart.

'I hope that this visit from your friends will help to make your Christmas happy.' He stared at her with an intentness that revealed nothing, and yet she sensed something within his mind that concerned her alone. She failed wholly to understand his attitude as he stood there by the window, superlatively groomed and attractive, his magnetic personality dominating the room. Hydee's heart twisted, the result of a futile longing for what was out of reach.

'I'm certainly looking forward to their visit,' she admitted. 'Ellie and I were such good friends when we shared the flat. It was she who saw me through that terrible time when my fiancé . . .' Abruptly she stopped, but of course it was too late to prevent the question.

'Your fiancé? You were once engaged?'

She shrugged resignedly. 'Yes, I was.'

'And?' Carlos shot a searching glance in her direction.

'He . . . he threw me over.' Colour rose as memory flooded in, colour born of humiliation.

Carlos's eyes grew hard, then narrowed. 'When did this happen?'

'About eighteen months ago. He fell in love with someone else. . . .' Again she shrugged her shoulders. 'It's of no importance now. I got over it.' She swallowed convulsively to clear her throat of the little ball of pain which had suddenly lodged there. 'One does get over these things in time.'

Carlos was silent, avoiding her eyes, and she realised that her confession had touched him deeply. It would not be unnatural for him to be thinking that, in effect, she had been rejected for a second time in favour of another woman. Did he feel a momentary twinge of compassion? she wondered when at length he met her gaze. The quiver of anger sw·eeping through her caused her to speak swiftly and without due thought.

'Don't you dare pity me, Carlos! I *hate* to be pitied! I have a wonderful friend in Gasper, so why should you pity me? I . . . I might marry him when our divorce comes through!' She stopped abruptly, dropping her lids against the smouldering fury that had leapt into the dark metallic pools of his eyes.

'Marry!' he said hoarsely. 'Marry Gasper?'

She shook her head, cursing herself for the loss of control which had resulted in that urge to hit out at him. 'Forget all about it—' she began, when he interrupted her.

'You seem so sure there's going to be a divorce,' he gritted. 'You know my attitude towards it.'

'You'd remain married and yet separated—you living in your country and I in mine?' When he did not answer, Hydee spoke again. 'I intend to leave you, Carlos,' she assured him quietly, her face pale and beautiful in its frame of gleaming dark hair, an ethereal quality about the translucent alabaster of her skin. Her limpid eyes were grave yet lit with the fire of determination, meeting those of her husband squarely, fearlessly, as she went on to add, 'Our marriage has collapsed, and will soon be a closed chapter in our lives. It would be degrading for us both if we lived together in the way we have been doing these past weeks. I blame myself,' she added with a sigh. 'It was a foolhardy thing to do, and if I had given it only a few days' thought, I'd have seen how impossible it would have been for it to work.'

'You mean . . . it couldn't have worked, whatever had happened?'

She stared, profoundly moved by something in his attitude rather than the words he had uttered.

'I don't understand. . . .' She felt a quiver of weakness in her legs, a tiny lurch in the region of her heart. 'You . . . you know why it hasn't worked.' She was tacitly referring to Arminda, but he let that pass.

'There are certain nonessentials to a successful marriage.'

'Love is not one of them, Carlos,' she returned softly. 'In fact, it's the first essential. Without it a marriage cannot possibly succeed.'

His gaze was inscrutable. 'This . . . this affection you have for my cousin—you sounded as if it was deep. . . .' His voice stopped as his teeth snapped together. Hydee's eyes widened to their fullest extent; she was denying the evidence of her ears even while the insistent hammering on her brain tapped out the word: *jealousy*.

Jealousy. . . . She shook her head, dazed by the incredible idea that had thrust itself into her consciousness. She looked at her husband, noting his dark countenance, the compression of his mouth, the flexed line of the jaw and the uncontrollable

175

rioting of a nerve in his throat. *If* it were jealousy, then surely she could exploit the situation.

'I certainly like Gasper very much,' she managed, feeling a liar because she was subtly inserting more emotion into her words than she felt.

'And he?' with a rasping inflection. 'He feels the same way about you?'

'Of course. We've known from the first that there's something rather special about our friendship.' That at least was true, she thought.

'Are you telling me you love Gasper?' he demanded. Hydee paused, unable to look him in the face and lie. Her hesitation told him far more than words ever could, and she heard a long drawn-out escape of breath, saw the curve of an enigmatic smile hover on his lips as he said, 'We shall leave it until after Christmas, Hydee, and then have a serious talk. Meanwhile, I have promised to act as if I . . .' He stopped, then rephrased his words. 'Between us we shall satisfy your friends that you are happy.'

The day before Christmas dawned sunny and comparatively warm, with the sky crystal clear except for a fine lacy veil of cirrus clouds floating over the terraced hillsides where the vineyards lay.

Hydee rose and went to the window, throwing wide the drapes to get a view of the gardens, dewy bright and colourful in the early-morning sun. She stretched luxuriously, her thoughts with Ellie and Ray, who had arrived the previous evening in time for dinner. Carlos had been especially gracious on greeting them, with the result that any fears which Ellie had still harboured about her friend had dissolved at once.

'He's marvellous!' Ellie had exclaimed when she and Hydee were alone for a short while just before dinner. 'You were right and I was wrong, that's for sure!'

Hydee had sighed a little, wondering why her recent optimism had so swiftly evaporated. She was having to assume a happiness and contentment she was far from feeling, because the more she dwelt on it, the more she felt she had been mistaken in suspecting her husband of jealousy. He had invited Arminda and her mother to the Christmas Eve party, so it was unlikely that he was thinking of giving her up.

Opening the bedroom window, Hydee stepped onto the balcony in her bare feet, forgetting everything but the sheer undiluted purity of the morning. New impressions crowded in—the pure light atmosphere, the jewelled foliage of the trees, the colourful sheen of the hillsides and the winding earthy path far down in the valley. Hydee stood a long while in deep appreciation of the tranquil panorama presented to her gaze; she seemed to have no sense of time, no urgency to begin the numerous tasks in front of her.

Half an hour later, when she was ready to go down to breakfast, she saw Ellie and Ray strolling in the garden hand in hand. A tiny sigh escaped her, but she was happy for them. Their future was rosy because of the love they had for each other.

Carlos was already in the breakfast salon when she arrived there, and the delicious smell of freshly cooked bacon and kidneys assailed her nostrils. Carlos smiled, and she responded, her spirits lifting because of his mood.

'Ellie and Ray are in the garden,' she informed

him, looking faintly troubled. 'I hope they won't keep you waiting too long, Carlos.'

'Don't apologise for your friends,' he said at once, a curve of wry humour on his lips. 'They're on their honeymoon and must do as they like.'

'Thank you,' she said simply, and sat down on the chair he had pulled out for her. He seemed to stay above her; she caught the fresh, almost exhilarating smell of after-shave mingling with newly laundered linen. Her hair moved. Had his chin touched it? Hydee caught her breath, tilting her head, and her eyes met his. Nerve centres quivered, blood pumped unevenly through her veins. Her whole being was vitally alive to his nearness and the fact that it was he alone who made it so.

'I've told Caterina to give the children their breakfast in the nursery this morning,' he said, moving at last to take a seat opposite her. 'I thought you and your friends could chat better without the interruption of the children.'

She threw him a glance of gratitude. She adored having the children with her but was pleased that on this special morning she could carry on an uninterrupted conversation with her friends.

They arrived within minutes, faces flushed and happy. Greetings exchanged, they sat down opposite one another, Ellie on Hydee's right and Ray on her left. The next hour was one of the most pleasant social interludes Hydee had ever spent in her life, partly because it was rather wonderful to be eating a meal with Ellie again but mainly because of Carlos's gracious manner with his guests . . . and his almost tender manner with his wife. And when Hydee caught his eyes unexpectedly, she gasped at what she saw in their dark metallic depths. Ellie saw it too, and her eyes widened. When Hydee looked at her, she was holding her fork in midair as if she had forgotten to carry it all the way to her mouth.

'Why didn't you tell me you'd fallen in love with each other?' Ellie demanded later when she and Hydee were alone in one of the smaller salons. She and Ray had met the children, and Ellie described them as 'rather special.' They took to Ray and insisted on dragging him off to see the Christmas tree and then they showed him the gardens and the swimming pool. 'He's just crazy about you!' Ellie added when her friend did not speak. 'And it's easy to see that you're just as crazy about him.'

'You think he . . . he cares?' The way Hydee asked that brought a frown to Ellie's forehead.

'What do you mean? It's as clear as that sky out there. He adores you!'

Hydee's nerves fluttered, and for a few tense moments she could only stare, her hands clasped tightly in her lap. Ellie waited, an anxious expression on her face. When at last Hydee did speak, it was to relate everything that had occurred, and she especially laid stress on Carlos's assertion that he cared deeply for Arminda.

'Gasper believes he's in love with her, too,' she added finally, but Ellie shook her head.

'A man doesn't look at a woman the way Carlos looks at you unless he loves her. I should know,' added Ellie with a tender smile after a tiny pause.

'I daren't let myself believe it, Ellie . . . and yet . . .'

'From what you've told me, he's fallen out of love with this Arminda—if he ever was in love with her—and fallen in love with you. In my mind there isn't one shadow of doubt.'

'I wish he'd talk to me now, instead of waiting,' sighed Hydee. 'This suspense is awful!'

'Forget the suspense,' advised her friend confidently. 'Carlos must have some reason for what he's doing, but I can assure you you'll not be returning to England after Christmas!'

'If only you could be right. . . .'

'I am right,' declared Ellie, then abruptly changed the subject, asking to be shown over the Palacio.

Hydee took her from one magnificent apartment to another, marvelling at the difference in herself, a difference resulting from her optimism that all was not lost after all.

'You really do act the marquesa very well,' Ellie said in tones of deep admiration. 'Anyone would think you'd been born to all this!'

Hydee gave a grimace and told her to wait until this afternoon, when the first of her husband's relatives would arrive.

'They dislike me intensely,' she went on, seeing no sense in trying to hide what would be so outstandingly clear before many more hours had passed. 'Carlos's sister has said quite openly that she considers me inferior.'

'She's . . . ?' Ellie stared in disbelief. 'But where are her manners?'

'They're sadly lacking, Ellie. And the others . . . I'm not going to bore you with their descriptions, because you'll soon be seeing them all for yourself. In the home of a Portuguese nobleman there's always a big party on Christmas Eve, when all his relatives converge on his house, where they stay for several days.'

'Sounds as if it'll be fun!'

Hydee had to laugh. 'It'll be different, Ellie, I'll grant you that.' She went on then to speak of Gasper, the only one of Carlos's relatives who had accepted her—and laughingly repeated his words about the plebeians being outnumbered.

'Tomorrow evening there's an even bigger party, when all the estate workers and their families come up to the Palacio. It's really a sort of tea party, mainly for the children, but everyone —adults as well—receives a present from the tree.'

'The tree's vast! I've never seen one of that size *inside* a house before!'

'It needs to be big because of the size of the room, but also because there are so many presents.'

'Hundreds of them, I noticed. Did *you* have to choose them and wrap them all?'

Hydee shook her head. 'No, the servants did that. I suppose Carlos chose the main presents himself, but he'd never have the time to go out and choose all you saw in the tree. I helped decorate the tree, of course, with the children, and Carlos helped, too. And then I had the help of Caterina and Jesuina for the process of tying on the presents.'

'You sound as if you enjoyed it.'

'It was a happy task, yes—especially as the children were dancing up and down with excitement all the time.'

'You're very lucky,' mused her friend. 'And to think, if you'd taken notice of me, you'd have had none of this.'

Hydee looked at her through faintly shadowed eyes. 'Ellie,' she said, a catch in her voice, 'none of it

181

could ever mean anything to me without the love of my husband.'

The Christmas Eve party was more in the nature of a traditional supper, and the main course of the meal was the national dish—*pacalhau*. There were other subtly spiced dishes, delectable fruits and vintage wine flowing all the time.

'I shall be tipsy!' exclaimed Ellie, turning from Hydee to Ray. 'Isn't this exciting?'

'It's a wonderful start to our honeymoon,' he agreed, smiling.

'What do you think about the relations?' from Gasper with a grin.

'Least said, soonest mended,' laughed Ellie. 'They looked at Ray and me as if we'd fallen off a garbage cart.'

'Ellie!' exclaimed Gasper. 'You'll have our august host hearing you!' But he was amused, and when his eyes met those of his cousin, they were alight with challenge.

However, the meal was a huge success, and immediately afterwards they were entertained by two men playing a guitar and a viola, and a beautiful young *fadista* who sang traditional ballads of sadness and the tragedies of life. One particular *fado* touched Hydee so deeply that she turned impulsively to her husband to ask if he would translate the words for her. 'It's incredible that she can move me so deeply when she's singing in a language I don't even understand!'

For a moment Carlos paused as if reluctant to comply with her request. However, he did translate, and Hydee learned that the ballad was the sad lament of a girl who had lost her lover to another, more beautiful woman. She sang of her loneliness, and as she ended the song, her voice fell almost to a whisper and there were tears in her eyes.

'It's . . . it's beautiful. . . .' Hydee turned again to Carlos, her own eyes bright, lashes stiff. The two men continued playing; Carlos took her hand to lead her onto the dance floor. For a full two minutes they had the floor to themselves, and as Hydee glanced around, she could not help but note the scowl on her sister-in-law's face and the compression of Arminda's pretty mouth. Hydee just had to say, 'Your people would be far happier if I weren't here, Carlos.'

He held her from him, and her heart fluttered at his expression.

'If they're not happy, they can keep away in future,' he said, the grim edge to his voice bearing no relation to the expression in his eyes, for it was one of tenderness not unmingled with regret, and there was a hint of humility there, too, which Hydee found unsettling because it seemed totally at odds with his proud personality.

She half-expected him to come to her room that night, but he had seemed very tired when she left him in the salon, where the family had gathered to arrange their shoes on the long wide mantelpiece beside those placed there earlier by the children, and she was tired, too. But if she had had any doubts left in her mind about his feelings for her, they must have been dispelled when on Christmas morning she took down her shoe and, opening the slender, velvet-lined box it contained, stared in wide-eyed wonderment at the set of exquisite jewellery that lay there—a necklace, bracelet and eardrops fashioned from flawless diamonds and emeralds. Both Ellie and Ray happened to be close, looking over her shoulder, and Ellie's loud 'Oh' of admiration attracted the attention of all the others present.

'How very beautiful,' from Arminda through whitened lips.

'Exquisite,' from Isobella, who automatically touched a huge diamond on her own finger.

'Delightfully feminine . . . and most fitting for our beautiful marquesa!' With a challenging glance shot in his cousin's direction, Gasper took Hydee by the arms, drew her to him, and kissed her on the cheek. 'Happy Christmas, Hydee!' he said for all to hear. And then, very softly, 'You made it! He's seen sense at last.' His lips brushed her cheek again before he moved aside.

Hydee turned to her husband, her eyes unnaturally bright. 'Thank you,' she murmured huskily. 'They're . . . so beautiful. . . .' Carlos came close, a smile in his eyes, Hydee's present to him in his hand. It was an exquisitely carved piece of netsuke.

'And thank you, dear,' he said gently. 'How did you know I collected netsuke? I don't believe I've ever mentioned it to you.'

'Gasper told me,' she answered, remembering how thrilled she had been on finding it. But as she had known nothing about netsuke, she had asked Gasper to go into the shop and look at it for her. She bought it after he had said it would be one of the prizes of his cousin's collection.

Gasper had been amazed that the shopkeeper, an ancient spinster known merely as Fernanda, had been able to get hold of such a high-quality piece of netsuke, which was a rare commodity anyway. However, it was just the present for Carlos, and Hydee had been delighted to find it.

'You like it?' She had to say something to break the silence as she watched Carlos turning it over in his hand.

'It's very lovely,' he replied. 'A most desirable addition to my collection.'

Lunch that day was exceptional, but the main event of Christmas Day in the home of a Portuguese *hidalgo* was always the party given for the estate employees and their families. This was the time for distributing the presents from the glittering tree, Carlos cutting them off and Hydee, helped by Ellie, giving them out.

'What a day!' Ellie exclaimed when, at almost midnight, she and Hydee managed to snatch a few minutes alone, having moved surreptitiously from the main salon to one of the smaller ones. All the estate workers had left with their families, and the house was comparatively quiet again. 'I shall never forget all this as long as I live!'

'Nor I,' agreed Hydee. 'It was really something, wasn't it?'

'Something to talk about for a long time to come.' They continued to chat for a while, and it was only when both were almost asleep that Ellie suggested they go to bed.

Once again Hydee wondered if Carlos would come to her, and this time she was not disappointed. He opened the door and stood there, fresh and cool after a shower, his hair damp, his long body clad in a dressing gown which appeared to have nothing underneath it. Hydee was by the dressing table brushing her hair. A smile illuminated her face as she stared at him in the mirror, then turned and stood waiting for him to speak. Instead, he moved towards her, reached out his hands and waited. Joyfully she

185

went to him, arms outstretched, and in seconds she was thrilling to his strong arms about her quivering body, his mouth cool and tender on her lips.

'There is so much to say, my darling, and yet I don't want to say it tonight.' He held her from him, eyes filled with tender amusement on noticing the battle going on within her as she strove to give him an answer. 'Woman's curiosity,' he mocked. 'It would appear it wins by a short head. For myself I'd rather make love and leave the more prosaic matters for the morning.'

She had to laugh, but explained, not without a certain measure of shyness, that she would enjoy his lovemaking much better if everything were cleared up first.

'How unromantic!' he jibed. 'In any case, it'll take so long that you'll be too tired.'

'Try me,' she returned, burying her face in his dressing gown. 'I'm not a bit tired.'

'Liar. I met Ellie on the landing and she said you'd both nearly fallen asleep downstairs.'

'I've wakened up since then.'

He lifted her chin, claiming her lips for a long moment, before, with a little shrug of resignation, he began to explain how he had come to be interested in Arminda.

'She was a friend of Isobella's, and I now feel sure that it was she who was the instigator of Arminda's move into this district. I admit I was attracted to Arminda; she became a regular visitor to my home and I to hers, with the natural result that my family concluded we'd get married. They knew I was more interested in acquiring a wife than another nanny. I'd had enough of nannies; I wanted my children to be loved. Well, it seemed that Arminda was a

suitable choice because she was so charming with
Luisa and Ramos, but somehow, neither of them
took to her. Then one day I happened to catch the
change in her expression after the children had burst
in on us when we were sitting together. I had the
impression of impatience—only fleetingly, because
Arminda instantly adopted her customary charm of
manner with them. I was troubled, though, and
watched her from then on. You know the rest. I
decided she was not suited to be a mother to my
children, but I still cared for her.' He stopped a
moment, silent in thought. 'I was still determined to
have a wife,' he continued presently. 'My first wife
was an exception, but in the main, Englishwomen
are exceedingly kind to children, so I decided to try
to find a suitable Englishwoman to be my wife.
Added to this, Ramos and Luisa speak the language
perfectly.' Again he stopped, then once again said
she knew the rest.

'You found me,' she inserted, unable to think of
anything else to say, and in any case, she wanted his
explanation to come to an end as quickly as possible.

'Yes, I found you,' he murmured, brushing her
lips before placing a kiss on the tip of her nose. 'To
resume, though, I felt guilty about Arminda and also
I still felt I cared deeply for her. Yet on reflection I
realise that I was never totally unaware of you as a
woman, and gradually I found myself wanting you.'
Faintly he smiled, kissing her cheeks because she
had blushed. But Hydee sensed his deep regret at
the cruel words he had used to her, saying he had
taken her because *she* had wanted it. 'As I don't
consider myself a fickle man, I suppose I had a
fixation about caring for Arminda,' Carlos went on
eventually. 'But I now realise that, from the moment

you came here, I was losing interest in her, and I also know that when I told you I cared deeply, it was not the truth, although, at the time, I believed it was, or wanted to believe it. Then there was the added complication of Gasper, whom you allowed to kiss you and with whom you seemed to be falling in love, and in fact you told me you would probably marry him when—'

'Oh, Carlos,' she cried, straining from him, 'don't bring that up! It wasn't true—really it wasn't!'

Carlos laughed then and drew her to his heart again. 'You've no need to tell me, sweetheart. I guessed you were trying to make me jealous—'

'That was afterwards, when I said I like Gasper very much and that we'd known from the first that there was something rather special about our friendship.'

'Well, it's of no more importance now than my own equally untrue statement that I cared deeply for Arminda,' He paused, because she had lifted her face, eyes shining, lips moistly glowing, inviting a kiss. 'As regards my being with Arminda in London,' continued Carlos sometime later, 'she and her mother had suffered financial losses of great magnitude; she believed she had been robbed and wanted me to look into some investments which she had over there. I agreed to help, feeling it was the least I could do, but refused to travel with her, owing to the possibility of gossip. Well, Isobella knew Arminda was going to London, knew, too, that I was to be there as well, so she made it her business to tell you about it. Gasper also knew, so he verified Isobella's statement, though without sharing her cruel intentions. It must have looked black against me but, believe me, dearest, I was not unfaithful to you.'

'I know, Carlos. When you hinted as much, I believed you rather than Isobella, and it helped, but I still had the idea that you could never fall in love with me.'

His eyes were tender as he said, 'I've been falling in love with you since the first day. I know that now. What finally made it hit me with some force was that night—'

'I know which night, Carlos,' she broke in swiftly. 'You were so loving with me.'

'And you with me, dearest.' He stopped and gave a small sigh. 'Arminda, like everyone else, knew the circumstances of our marriage, so Arminda continued to believe I loved her. Well, after that wonderful night I knew I must tell her it was my wife whom I loved, but I was reluctant to upset her before Christmas, hence my saying that you and I would talk afterwards. However, as things turned out, I was unable to hide my love from you, and Arminda tackled me, so I admitted it. She took it very well but told me that she and her mother will be leaving the district within the next few months.'

'I feel sorry for her, Carlos.'

'So do I, but it was fate that she and I did not marry. You, my beloved, were waiting for me.'

'Yes, waiting for my Prince Charming. . . .' She smiled, offering her lips. 'Kiss me, dear Carlos,' she whispered huskily—and within seconds she was swept into a wild torrent of passion that left her breathless and limp in his arms, joyfully submissive, his for the taking.

Silhouette Romance

IT'S YOUR OWN SPECIAL TIME

Contemporary romances for today's women.
Each month, six very special love stories will be yours
from SILHOUETTE. Look for them wherever books are sold
or order now from the coupon below.

$1.50 each